Witch School
Book 1

Miss Moffat's Academy
for
Refined Young Witches

Katrina Kahler

Table of Contents

Chapter One

The shrill sound of the ambulance was deafening as it pulled up outside. But at least it had drowned out the sound of the panicked mothers as they hovered around the boy frozen stiff in the middle of the room.

Fortunately, Charlotte's mother had narrowly beaten the ambulance to the birthday party. She took in the scene and knew exactly what to do.

This is the moment that Charlotte's life changed forever...

It all started at Charlotte's next-door neighbor's birthday party and the silly thing is that she didn't even want to be there.

There were bunches of balloons scattered around the room, all in varying shades of pink. A banner with the message 'happy birthday' on it took up half of the far wall, and a group of adults stood to the side of the room, sipping on tea and stuffing their faces with leftover sandwiches.

Charlotte Smyth sat crossed-legged on the floor, in between a girl who kept rubbing her nose onto the back of her sleeve and a flat-haired boy who'd already won at apple bobbing and musical statues. She felt foolish being there playing party games at the age of eleven, but it was a family friend's party and she didn't want to upset the birthday girl, so she went along with it. Charlotte took the pink wrapped parcel off the nose-rubbing girl and that's when the One Direction song stopped playing.

'That's not fair, SHE CHEATED!' the flat-haired boy screamed.

'No, I didn't,' Charlotte replied, before she ripped the layer of paper off the parcel, revealing another layer of paper and a lollipop.

'You held onto it for ages,' he said as he snatched the lollipop out of the paper.

'Hey, that's mine.' Charlotte tried to get the lollipop back, but he kept moving it out of her reach.

'Ed give it back, the music stopped on Charlotte,' a girl who sat opposite them said.

'Yeah, give it back Ed,' another boy said.

'It's okay, I have spares,' one of the viewing adults came tottering over and pulled a lollipop from her cardigan pocket then passed it to Charlotte.

The boy smirked at Charlotte before the music restarted, and he snatched the parcel out of her lap and reluctantly passed it to the poor child who sat next to him.

Pass-the-parcel finished, and Charlotte stood up and was about to walk away when this most annoying boy sarcastically wisecracked. 'Your hair is so curly.'

Charlotte looked up to see the flat-haired boy smirking at her. 'It's stupid, you look like a giant fuzz ball.'

'Shut-up,' she growled back.

'What was that, fuzz ball? I couldn't hear you under all that fuzz.'

Charlotte stared at the grinning boy, annoyed and angry by his comments.

'Yeah well, you're a...' It was then that she realized that the boy wasn't moving, he was still grinning, but his entire body was still. She waved her hand in front of the boy's face, but he didn't blink.

'Stop messing about, it's not funny,' she poked his arm with her finger and watched in alarm as his rigid body fell backwards onto the floor.

A nearby girl let out a scream and a couple of the adults came rushing over.

'Edward, Edward darling, say something,' a woman gently shook him. 'He's not moving. He's rigid!'

'Musical statues is over, buddy,' a man bent down by the boy and tried bending his arms, only they would not move. 'What the fudge,' he let go of Ed and took a step back. 'He's frozen solid, he's a statue.'

'Don't just stand there Keith, ring an ambulance,' the woman snapped at him.

The man fiddled in his pocket for his phone, finally finding it and calling for emergency help. Within minutes they could hear the ambulance approaching and just as it pulled up outside...a pretty, well-dressed woman, with hair as frizzy as Charlotte's rushed over to the boy and bent down in front of him.

'He's quite alright, he just needs a glass of water,' she said to the boy's mother.

'He's not all right, HE'S FROZEN SOLID!' she sobbed.

'Please, a drink,' the frizzy haired woman forced a smile.

Ed's mother asked another woman to go and get the water and to be quick as her precious son was dying.

'Some space please,' the woman said to the crowd of onlookers, and they all took a reluctant step backwards. She bent over Ed and whispered some words.

With a cough and a splutter Ed sat up, he shook out his limbs and repeatedly blinked his eyes before focusing them on Charlotte.

'Her, it was her!' he pointed straight at Charlotte.

'I didn't do anything.'

'Yes, you did, you did this to me. I saw you do it!'

The woman hurried back over with the glass of water and held it up to Ed's lips.

'It's okay sweetie,' his mother wrapped her arms around him.

'It was her, Mother, I saw her do it.'

'With the utmost respect I don't see how my daughter could have caused such a thing to have happened,' the frizzy haired woman stood-up and walked over to Charlotte. 'We're leaving,' she whispered to her.

As Charlotte followed her mom across the room she felt everyone's gaze on her as they gossiped amongst themselves. She'd been angry with Ed and she'd wanted him to stop teasing her, but she didn't see how she could have caused him to freeze. She came to the conclusion that he must have eaten something funny, as people didn't just freeze solid for no reason.

Her mom was silent as they walked home, but Charlotte didn't mind this. As they walked, she wondered if she'd ever be invited to a party again.

It wasn't until later that day that Charlotte's mom called her into the kitchen and gestured for her to take a seat next to her at the circular table.

'Hi sweetie, I want to talk to you about what happened earlier at the party,' her mom said, her voice gentle.

'I didn't touch him Mom, he was teasing me, but I didn't do anything.'

'I know that you didn't intend to do anything but that doesn't mean you didn't,' she sighed before continuing. 'Your father doesn't know this because he's an ordinary, a human, but I'm a witch.'

'A w-what?'

'When I was a child I found that I could do things, extraordinary things and it appears that you also have powers,' she placed a hand on top of Charlotte's. 'It's nothing to be afraid of, actually it's exciting, but you need to go somewhere where you can be properly trained so that nothing like what happened at the party ever happens again. As I said before, your dad knows nothing about witches. He is an ordinary. So, this has to be our secret.'

'I didn't mean to do anything to that boy, although he was horrible. I'm not a w-witch,' Charlotte pulled her hand free from under her mom's and folded her arms.

Her mother glanced around the kitchen to confirm they were alone before she looked at the unlit candle in the center of the room, then clicked her fingers. A bright flame immediately appeared and gently flickered. Charlotte stared at it open-mouthed before turning her gaze to her mom.

'You're a witch, Charlotte, just like me. Ever since you were a toddler, I have watched you manipulating objects,' she gently grabbed Charlotte's shoulders and looked directly at her. 'There's two possible boarding schools where you can go to learn to control your powers. Witchery College and Miss Moffat's Academy for Refined Young Witches. My preferred choice for you is the latter, I contacted them earlier and they have a space. You're very lucky to have this opportunity, you will make lots of friends and learn so much,' she smiled.

'Then why don't you go to it,' Charlotte snapped. 'Sorry, it's just all a bit much.'

'It's okay sweetie, I understand. We'll talk more about this tomorrow but remember what I said about your father, he doesn't know about witches. He thinks that you're going to a normal boarding school, so please don't tell him otherwise. Ordinaries have a hard time grasping the magical world, which is why we like to keep it a secret from them.'

'Okay,' Charlotte nodded.

***

That morning she'd been a normal eleven-year-old girl but now everything had changed. She thought back to all the times in her life when odd things had happened, like the time when the broken nib of her pencil reappeared so that she could finish her school exam. There was also the time when the only yoghurt left was a loathed cherry flavor one, but when she went to eat it, it tasted of strawberries. But she'd never turned someone into a statue before, maybe she really was different to the other children, maybe she really was a witch.

Chapter Two

It was muggy in the car and Charlotte's hair was stuck to her damp forehead. She wanted to open the window, but her mom didn't like the noise that it made when the wind came through the gap. The air-con was on, but this didn't seem to help much, and Charlotte knew better than to open the window. Her mom was almost as anxious about today as she was, the fact that she'd caught her re-washing the dishes for the second time after breakfast verified this.

For the last few weeks Charlotte's mom had been dropping the new school into conversation wherever she could. A fact which had made Charlotte more apprehensive, it was also hard not being able to discuss it properly with her mom when her dad was around. She felt as if she was being thrown into a snake pit with no knowledge of which ones were poisonous.

They were on their way to Miss Moffat's Academy and Charlotte knew that there was no going back.

'Will we be there soon?' she asked, wiping back a strand of hair off her sticky face.

'In about an hour sweetie, we'll stop off and grab a drink on-route.'

'If I don't like this school do I have to stay there?'

'You will like it, you're fortunate to have been offered a place.'

'Maybe they should have given it to someone else,' she said under her breath.

'Charlotte, it will be fine, you just have to be yourself and you'll settle right in.'

'Okay,' she sighed, the concern still sitting in the pit of her stomach.

Charlotte turned her head and stared out of the window, watching as her old life blurred past her and her new, unknown one drew evermore closer.

***

After parking the car and her mom yet again going on about how great the school was, they both got out of the car. Charlotte followed her mom down a pathway surrounded by trees and they soon arrived in a clearing where a large maze of green lay in front of them.

'This is the furthest I can take you,' her mom said, as she leaned down and hugged her daughter.

'B-but it's a maze, I don't know where I'm going,' Charlotte looked at the narrow path between the high walls of greenery.

'It's the Entry Maze. It's part of the initiation process.'

'I'll get lost Mom, I can't do it.'

'Yes, you can,' her mom grabbed her arms and looked directly at her. 'You can do this Charlotte, just follow your instinct.'

'But it's so big and I don't know where I'm going,' tears dripped down Charlotte's cheeks.

'You'll know when you find it,' she wiped away one of the tears before she squeezed Charlotte tight. 'Now go before you set me off,' she forced back her own tears as she kissed her on the top of her head.

"Okay Mom, I love you,' Charlotte forced a smile before she nervously walked towards the maze entrance, looking back once at her mom and giving a wave before she continued up the path and into the unknown.

Charlotte had never been keen on mazes, not since she'd ended up separated from her parents in a crop maze when she was five. A random family had stumbled upon her, led her out of it, and reunited her with her parents. She knew that this time no one would come to rescue her and that she was in this on her own.

She came across yet another dead-end and looked around her, a panicked feeling growing in her stomach. The midday sun was beating down and she didn't know where to go or what to do. Sitting down on the ground, she regained her breath as she tried to calm herself and figure out what to do next.

'You can do this,' she said to herself, before she closed her eyes tightly and murmured a desperate plea. 'Please, I don't know where to go, I need some help.'

Charlotte opened her eyes to see a ball of light in front of her. At first she wasn't sure if it was the heat or her anxiety causing her to imagine things but upon blinking, the ball of light remained in sight. The light began to move forwards, so she followed it as it weaved through the passageways, eventually stopping at another dead-end. Only this one wasn't like the other ones she'd previously found, as it contained a large tree. It was so large that Charlotte wondered how she hadn't seen it above the maze walls. It was as luscious green in color as the hedgerows were.

The tree shook which made Charlotte jump off her feet and then six green faces appeared amongst the foliage.

'Hello child,' the first face said, which caused Charlotte to become even more alarmed. This wasn't like one of the normal trees that were in the park near her house as she'd never heard them speak.

'We will ask you a question each, answer them correctly to gain access to the Academy,' the second face said.

'Don't worry, I'm sure you'll pass with flying colors,' the second face gave a friendly chuckle.

'Let's begin with an easy one. What's your name?' the first face asked.

'Ch-Charlotte Symth,' she croaked out.

'Correct,' the first face boomed.

'What is the color of a witch's hat?' the second face asked.

'Erm, black.'

'Correct.'

'What is the best mode of transport for a witch?' the third face asked.

'A broomstick,' she said confidently, beginning to think that these questions were a breeze.

'What is a witch's preferred pet?' the fourth face said.

'Erm, a frog, no an owl.'

'Incorrect,' the voice boomed, and Charlotte felt the tears well up in her eyes. She wondered if that was her only chance and she'd failed? 'Don't worry child, you can try again.'

She thought hard about what it could be and then she recalled the books her mom had read to her as a kid, about a clumsy witch and her magic world.

'A black cat.'

'Correct.'

'What do witches brew potions in?'

'Erm, a pot, no a cauldron.'

'Correct.'

'Nearly there, only this question to go. See if you can solve this riddle: What is a witch's favorite subject?' the sixth face asked.

Charlotte bit on the side of her lip as she thought about this. She'd never been good at riddles as she tended to over-think them. She took a deep breath and tried to think carefully, hoping that she'd be allowed a few chances to get it right.

'Potions.'

'Incorrect,' the sixth face boomed.

'Oh, erm flying.'

'Incorrect.'

'Okay,' she rolled her eyes back as she tried to think what it could be. She thought about what witches were famous for liking; magic, their pets, turning people into rodents and spells. They liked spells. 'Is it spelling?'

'Correct,' the sixth face said, and all the faces began to laugh in unison before the tree shook and the leaves flew into the sky, reforming as large leafy elephants.

'Cool,' she mouthed.

The maze vanished in front of her and in its place appeared a large field.

'Follow us,' the elephants said, before they began to plod along in front of her.

Charlotte did as they said, wondering what she'd have to do next. Suddenly a hole appeared beneath her and before she could do anything about it she felt herself falling. She landed on her feet in front of four life-sized stone statues of warriors on a platform. Behind them was a large castle. Could this be the Academy? She found herself annoyed at the elephants for coming across as nice and then luring her down that hole. They could have at least given her some warning.

'Is anyone home? Please can you let me in?' she shouted out, as she looked around for a door.

There was a loud clacking sound and Charlotte looked up to see the four statues pulling themselves down from their platform and walking over to her in their armor, with varying weapons in their hands as they circled her.

'What are you doing here?' one of the warriors asked, as he pulled his sword out of its case.

'I am, erm, I am a student here. I was in the maze and now I'm looking for the entrance.'

'An entrance,' the warrior laughed, before he turned to the warrior by him. 'You hear that Lancelot; she's looking for the entrance.'

'Please, the elephants, they brought me here. Well, they led me to the hole, and I fell and-'

'Enough, you're giving me a headache,' a warrior holding a

shield said.

'I can't hear myself think,' the third warrior said.

'Come on, this is enough,' the warrior known as Lancelot said.

'Spoilsport,' the first warrior said.

'Come on, you know if he doesn't get his way he will go on and on and on and on about it,' the fourth warrior said.

'Yes, you're right,' the first warrior sighed. 'Very well, go on.'

'We've been expecting you,' the fourth warrior laughed, which caused the others to laugh too.

'Ignore those fools,' a squeaky voice said. She looked up to see several bats flying above her head. 'Follow us,' they squeaked.

By this stage she didn't even question the fact that the bats were talking. She simply followed them, eager and grateful to escape the stone warriors.

'Follow us, follow us,' they squeaked, as they flew straight through the solid stone wall beside the warriors' platform.

Charlotte abruptly stopped and stared in disbelief, not understanding how they traveled through the wall. She thought that only ghosts could travel through walls, not witches. She wondered if the bats were tricking her and if perhaps they were ghosts instead. She didn't want to bash into the wall and then be laughed at.

'Hurry up and follow us,' the bats squeaked out as they flew back out of the wall and then flew back through it again.

Taking a deep breath, she took a few steps forwards before she paused in front of the mass of concrete and stared up at it, hoping that a door would appear and make things simpler.

'I can do this,' she said under her breath, before taking another step forwards so that she was almost touching the solid looking surface. She was about to reach out and touch it when one of the bats flew back out and flapped its wings beside her.

'No, you have to walk through it.' It's squeak was decisive. 'Hurry, hurry, you have to come now.'

Charlotte took one last look around her. She knew that she had to do it then or not at all, so she stepped through the wall.

Chapter Three

Pink Persian carpets covered the central part of the marbled floors that were under Charlotte's feet as she stood in the large, high ceilinged entrance hall.

She stopped by her bags that were there waiting for her and looked at the various spiral staircases that were in front of her, the banisters gold. Huge portraits of women in witches' hats and holding broomsticks were hanging on the grand looking walls and there was an overwhelming smell of rose petals.

Charlotte had never been anywhere as impressive as this

before and she found herself staring at it open-mouthed.

'Follow us, follow us,' the bats squeaked, before they flew down and picked up her bags with their feet and flew them up one of the staircases.

Charlotte wondered how they were strong enough to carry her bags but then again they could talk, so being extraordinarily strong seemed minor in comparison. She followed them up the staircase and past a large gold bust that was standing by the wall.

They led her through a gilded golden door and into a room that was about four times the size of her bedroom at home. There were four large, bronze framed beds in the rooms, each with an array of pillows in creams and golds and an ivory blanket folded at the end of the light grey colored duvet.

The bats placed her bags down in front of the bed furthest from the door, before they fluttered out of the room, closing the door behind them.

An owl appeared and perched on the windowsill by the open window and it watched Charlotte intently as she looked around the room.

Apart from the beds, the only other items in the room were an intricately carved ornate gold mirror and an enormous wooden wardrobe.

'Don't open the wardrobe,' the owl hooted.

'Why not?' she asked, wondering why the wardrobe had been put there if she couldn't use it.

'Don't open the wardrobe,' the owl repeated, before it flew off outside.

Charlotte sat down on her bed and wondered what she was supposed to do next. The castle was so massive and daunting; she decided that she'd just wait there until someone told her what she should do. She certainly did not want to try exploring and risk getting lost.

The door opened and the bats flew in carrying bags, followed by a girl in a creamy white dress, with chin length, wavy dark-blonde hair. The bats flew over to the bed by the window and put the bags down in front of it.

'Hi, I'm Stef,' she smiled, as she studied the room.

'Charlotte. Pleased to meet you Stef.'

'So, we're going to need rules for this bedroom gig to work. No sitting on other beds or touching each other's stuff!'

The door opened and again the bats flew in carrying bags, this time followed by a smiling girl, with curly blond hair.

'Hi, I'm Gerty,' she looked around excitedly. 'This place is so cool! I've never seen a castle this big before. And the bats actually talk.'

'How old are you?' Stef put her hands on her waist as she looked questioningly at the young girl.

'They don't normally accept students until they're eleven, but they let me in a year early because I'm good at magic,' she said without pausing for breath

'That's cool,' Charlotte said.

'I don't think it's a good idea for a ten-year-old to be here, from what I hear the lessons are challenging and a ten-year-old doesn't have the same maturity as an eleven-year-old.' Stef commented with a smug expression.

'It's only a year's difference,' Charlotte said.

'I'm so excited,' Gerty continued, ignoring Stef's comment. 'I've not been able to sleep properly in days. I wonder what lesson we'll have first?' Gerty fell back onto her bed and began to pull her body up with her hands as she bounced on the firm surface.

'Do you think anyone else will come and take that bed?' Stef asked curiously, as she gestured to the spare bed.

'I don't know,' Charlotte replied.

'Hopefully, it's just us because it'll give us more space,' Stef walked over to the wardrobe. 'At least we have this to put our clothes in.'

'I wouldn't open that, there was an owl here and it said not to open it.'

'Whatever,' Stef rolled her eyes before pulling open the
doors.

A black hole of intense force sucked Stef forwards, she
grabbed onto the inner side of the wardrobe and clung on
tightly as her body was turned horizontal. Charlotte and
Gerty both rushed over to her and each grabbed one of Stef's

arms, pulling as hard as they could.

A pretty girl with long blond hair tied into a high ponytail and wearing a knee length satin black skirt and a fitted white blouse that emphasized her slim waist, stepped into the room, a long silver wand in hand.

'Newbies,' she tutted, before she waved her wand in the girls' direction. 'Entario.'

Stef was thrown back into the room and she landed on the floor with a loud thump, her hair a mess and her dress blown up around her waist so that her old knickers with a hole by the waistband were on show. She immediately jumped up onto her feet, her cheeks flushed as she flattened down her dress and then tried to smooth down her hair.

Charlotte and Gerty both giggled and Stef stared at them sternly, which caused them both to fall silent.

'I am Molly McDonald, the head prefect,' she tapped the small silver triangular pin on her blouse, the words 'head prefect' written on it in italic black font. 'I am here to welcome you all to Miss Moffat's Academy, we are renown for being one of the most successful schools for witches in the world and you're all very lucky to be here. Don't squander this opportunity that you've been given. Also, it is of the utmost importance that you always follow the rules and instructions that have been given to you.' She glanced towards Stef who was looking embarrassed.

'Oh, there's still one more girl to come to this room,' she turned and said after she'd reached the door. 'Alice Smithers.'

'What's she like?' Gerty asked.

'You'll have to wait and see,' she shrugged, a smirk on her face, as she left the room.

'Are you okay?' Charlotte asked Stef.

'Yeah, fine,' she said defensively.

'Wasn't Molly so pretty? I want to be that pretty. Do you think I'll be able to cast a spell to make myself look like her?' Gerty asked.

'I think it'll be awhile before you learn powerful spells, I mean you are only ten,' Stef replied.

'You're already pretty, Gerty, you don't need to look like Molly,' Charlotte said.

'Thanks, I think you're both really pretty too and I love your hair,' she replied, which caused Charlotte to instinctively pat down her hair.

'Yeah, I suppose you look okay,' Stef shrugged.

'You guys are so nice. I hope Alice is nice too.'

'Yeah, me too,' Charlotte said, not wanting to be stuck in a room with someone she didn't like. Gerty was giggly and excitable and Stef was confident and blunt, but Charlotte liked them both and hoped that the other girl would fit in as well.

A loud bell rang out which startled Charlotte as she looked at the other girls. Just then the owl swooped into the room.

'Follow me to the meeting room,' the owl hooted, and the girls nodded before following it out of the room.

They were led down the spiral staircase and along the wide

hallway until they got to an arched doorway. As they walked closer, the doors opened inwards and the owl flew off. They stepped into the meeting room that was full of rows of chairs, most of which had students sitting on them. The room was alive with excited voices and Charlotte and Gerty followed Stef over to some free seats in one of the middle rows.

There was a raised platform in front of them with an impressive burgundy and gold armchair. The chair had an oval backrest that had massive dragon's wings attached to the sides.

'I've never seen this many witches before,' Gerty said, as she peered over her shoulder. 'It's so exciting.'

'How long do you think we'll have to sit here for?' Stef asked, as she restlessly tapped her fingers against the frame of her seat.

'It shouldn't be long,' Charlotte replied, looking up at the grey-bricked walls that had a row of colored shields displayed on them.

This whole experience was a new one for Charlotte and she wondered what was going to happen next. She was curious to find out what it would be but really hoped that she wouldn't have to solve any more riddles.

Chapter Four

The doors into the room opened and the room fell silent as dozens of bats flew up the aisle in-between the seats. Behind the bats flew a beautiful woman who was on a black handled broomstick with flickers of gold flashing vividly along its length. She hovered by the armchair and elegantly stepped off her broom, before making it float beside her.

Her long chestnut colored hair sat in cone shaped funnels at the sides of her head and her pale skin was clear of any blemishes. She stared towards the girls with eyes as dark as black sapphires, clutching authoritatively to her fur trimmed luxurious looking cloak.

Then, with a welcoming smile, she sat down on the chair and placed her arms elegantly on the rests.

'Hello students, new and old, I am Miss Moffat, the head-witchress and founder of this academy. I established it over four-hundred-years ago and regard it as my greatest achievement. Many well-renown witches have attended here, including Ivy Glossington who developed the famous chant to ward off trolls and Fiona Fitzgerald who wrote the best-selling *Witches Of The World* books.

This school is notorious for being one of the best of its kind, so for all the new students here today you should feel very privileged to have been offered a place here. I advise you all to make the most of this wonderful opportunity and not waste it. Each and every one of you now represents this school and what we stand for. Knowledge is what this school feeds on and from it can come greatness...but don't be fooled into thinking this can be achieved without hard work and one-hundred-per-cent effort. Many longed for a place here and didn't succeed. They're now forced to attend Witchery College, most-famous for its long line of witches who dabble in the dark arts, something that is thoroughly frowned upon at this academy.

When you have finished your education, you will graduate with the finest moral upstanding and most advanced skills in the magical community, skills which are considered-'

The doors creaked open, followed by footsteps. Miss Moffat was scowling so everyone else turned to see what had happened. Standing there in a green and yellow sequined dress and with her mousy brown hair under a witch's hat, was a young girl.

'Good afternoon, sorry I'm a tad late. My bags are outside, could you ask the servants to collect them for me.' Her voice was confident and assured and she was clearly unfazed by all the eyes on her. Everyone stared open-mouthed, amazed at her rudeness.

'And who, are you?' Miss Moffat asked.

'I am Alice, Alice Smithers. I presumed you would have known that.'

'You presumed wrong,' Miss Moffat replied.

Alice was about to say something else when Molly rushed over to her and led her over to Charlotte and the others.

'These are your room-mates,' Molly said.

'Oh, I'll be wanting my own room.'

'You have to share, everyone else your age shares a room,' Molly said, before she walked back over to her seat, leaving Alice standing there looking begrudgingly at the girls.

The only empty seat was next to Stef and that meant Alice would have to squeeze past Gerty and Charlotte to get to it, but it was clear that she wasn't willing to do this. Aware that everyone was staring, Charlotte gently nudged Stef's arm and motioned for her to move along. At first Stef shook her head and folded her arms but Charlotte furrowed her eyebrows with insistence. Stef let out an exaggerated sigh before she moved onto the next seat. Charlotte and Gerty both shuffled along as well which meant that Alice could sit down at the end of the row.

'As I was saying, it is at this Academy where you shall learn skills which are considered greatly valuable in the magical society. Your final goal for your education at this esteemed Academy is for all of you, even those of you who are rude enough to interrupt me, is to develop your powers in order to become refined young witches and learn to use your powers for the good of everybody, including ordinaries.

'There is a strict code of conduct at this Academy that you must follow.' Miss Moffat continued in a strict tone.

Dozens of scrolls flew in the door and floated in the air before the students.

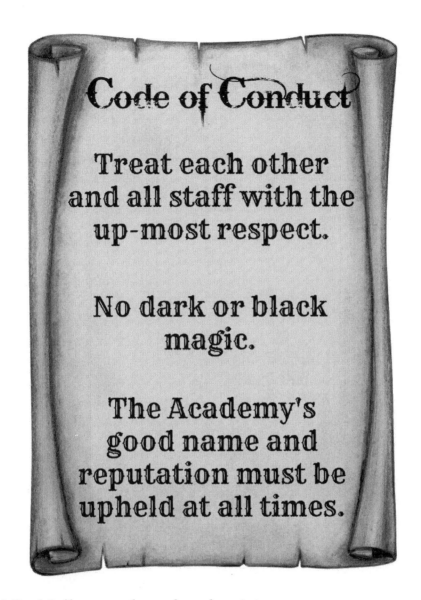

Code of Conduct

Treat each other and all staff with the up-most respect.

No dark or black magic.

The Academy's good name and reputation must be upheld at all times.

Miss Moffat went through each point.

'You must all treat each other and the members of staff with respect.' Her eyes focused on Alice as she made this statement.

'No dark or black magic will be tolerated in this Academy.'

'The Academy's reputation as a school for refined young witches is to be upheld at all times.'

'It'd be easier if she just laid down the rules, you know like lights out at 9pm and no running in the hall,' Gerty whispered to Charlotte, which caused her to giggle before putting her finger to her lips to signal for her to be quiet. It was then that Alice stuck her arm into the air but didn't wait to be asked to speak.

'Excuse me miss, those rules are fairly general, do you have any more specific ones?' she blurted out what everyone else was thinking, but that no one else dared to ask.

'This is not a day nursery for babies, you need to live by this code of conduct and make wise choices in the things you do and how you conduct yourself whilst at this Academy. There will be consequences for anyone who disobeys these rules. I was hoping that I wouldn't have to point this out today, but it appears that it may be necessary.

1st offence- a wart will appear on your face.

2nd- Your nose will grow, by how much is determined by the severity of your misadventure.

3rd- Your laugh shall change to that of a witch's cackle.

4th- Your skin shall turn green.

5th- Your eyes shall turn bright red and bloodshot.

6th- The final warning. The word naughty shall appear on your forehead and will remain there for an entire month.

The severity and timing of these punishments will depend on the code of conduct violation. In other words, the naughtier you are, the worse the consequence.'

Alice once again lifted up her hand.

'Yes Miss Smithers?' Miss Moffat said in a sarcastic tone.

'What happens if you are naughty after the sixth consequence?'

'Then you shall be expelled from this Academy and shall have to attend the lowly rated public-school Witchery College, headed by Mistress Ravenshawk,' she shuddered.

The girls all looked around at each other and exchanged knowing glances. It was clear that no one wanted to mess up, especially if it meant the consequence that Miss Moffat had threatened. Charlotte noticed that even Alice had gone quiet and lowered her gaze at the mention of Witchery College.

Charlotte found herself wondering how many students had been expelled and if Mistress Ravenshawk was as terrifying as she sounded, although she hoped that she'd never end up as a student at her school to find out.

'Go back to your room and unpack and get ready for dinner. If you're new here and unsure of the way back to your rooms then call for a bat and one will promptly arrive to guide you,' Miss Moffat stood up and got onto her broomstick. All the girls watched as she flew towards the now opened doors and left the room.

The hall instantly erupted into noise as all the girls began talking to each other.

'I know the way to the room,' Stef said, as she stood up and pushed her way past the others to get to the end of the row.

'Mind where you're treading with your big feet, these shoes are one-of-a-kind,' Alice demanded.

'Come on guys,' Stef ignored Alice's comment.

They all stood and joined Stef, following the crowd of girls out of the hall, excited at the prospect of their futures in this school.

Chapter Five

It turned out that Stef did remember the way back to the room and Charlotte tried to memorize the route, hoping that she wouldn't get lost when she was in the castle alone. The four of them walked inside and Gerty fell down onto her bed and swung her legs out over the side of it.

'Did you know that Miss Moffat is over four-hundred-years old? She looks amazing doesn't she and her hair, it's so beautiful and shiny. I think I might grow my hair that long and maybe when I'm older I'll dye it the same color as hers,' Gerty said excitedly.

'How can she be that old?' Charlotte asked.

'By magic of course,' Stef snorted.

'I'm new to this magic world so I didn't know.'

'That's okay, I can teach you,' Gerty smiled.

'Thanks, I'd like that.'

'I'll have that bed by the window,' Alice said, as she walked over to Stef's bed and sat down on it.

'Erm, no you won't, that bed's already been claimed by me. First come, first served,' Stef said.

'I should have my own room. Don't the staff here know who I am?' Alice was looking like she was going to be a king-sized pain!

'Clearly not,' Stef rolled her eyes.

'If I can't have my own room then I should at least get to pick which bed I have, and I want this one.'

'Well you can't have it because it's mine,' she strutted over to her bed, her hands on her hips. 'That one's yours, over by the bathroom.'

'I'm not having that one, it's the worst placed bed in the room,' Alice argued.

'Your bags are by it, see,' she pointed over to the large pile of bags that were by the bed. 'So that one's yours and this one is mine. You're currently sitting on my bed,' she smirked.

'This is ridiculous, rest assured that my parents will be hearing about this,' she abruptly hopped off the bed and stormed across the room and out of the door.

Stef sneaked over to the door and peered around it, followed by Gerty and Charlotte. They watched Alice storm off down the hallway.

'Where's she going?' Charlotte asked.

'Probably to ring up Mommy and Daddy and complain about the awful treatment she's been receiving here,' Stef put on a posh voice.

Gerty and Charlotte shared a look as if to say that Stef had gone too far, and Stef caught sight of it.

'Relax, she'll be back but she needed to know her place,' she walked away from the door. 'Don't worry about Alice, she'll be fine.'

Charlotte went back over to her bed and rummaged through her bags. She wanted to unpack but didn't know where she was supposed to put her clothes…seeing as the wardrobe was off limits. She wondered why the wardrobe was there when it couldn't be used. It was annoying as it was so huge, all four of them would have been able to fit their clothes into it.

She looked over at Stef who had pulled a separate draw from out under her bed and was filling it with piles of her clothes. Charlotte found that there was a draw under her bed too, so she pulled it out and began to sort out her clothes. She found herself wondering where Alice had gone and when she'd come back. She didn't want any more bickering to happen between Stef and Alice but they were both strong personalities so she doubted their room would become a calm zone anytime soon. At least all this drama kept her distracted from thinking about home and about how much she was missing her mom and dad.

Charlotte was still unpacking her belongings when Alice huffed her way back into the room, followed by two similar looking girls, one wearing black and the other had a white tunic on and both of them wore a triangular silver pin boasting the word 'prefect'. The most noticeable difference in their appearance was that one girl was a couple of inches taller than the other one.

'I'm Sonya and this is my sister Silvia, we're prefects here at the Academy. According to Alice, someone's stolen her bed,' the taller girl said.

'Erm, no they haven't,' Stef folded her arms. 'Alice was the last one into the room and therefore she should have the bed that's left.'

'I am from a very important witching family called The Smithers, who I'm sure you've heard of, so I should have priority. And according to my measurements I have 29 and a half inches less space than the rest of you and that is NOT fair!

'If you were last in the room then you'll have to put up with the bed that's left, I don't see the problem,' Sonya said, as she flicked her long blonde hair behind her ears.

'The problem is that it's not the bed I want,' Alice complained.

'Well you should have got here earlier then,' Stef said.

'Alice, we suggest that you calm down and try to fit in,' Silvia said, before they both turned around and headed out of the room.

'But that's not fair. Don't you know who I am?' Alice shouted to their backs but neither of them turned around. 'Fine,' she said under her breath, as she walked over to her bed and lifted her bags on top of it.

'Where are the servants? It's positively awful that I'm expected to unpack this myself.'

'Just get on with it.' Stef rolled her eyes. She'd finished her own packing and was now lying on her bed.

Alice grabbed a handful of clothes and walked over to the wardrobe. Stef smirked in Charlotte's direction at the sight of what Alice was doing. Charlotte looked from Alice to the wardrobe and knew that she should say something. However annoying Alice was, Charlotte didn't think that she deserved to be sucked into that black hole. As Alice got closer to the wardrobe…even Stef's grin faltered, and Charlotte opened her mouth to warn her.

'Don't open that, it's like a wind tunnel in there, it'll suck you in,' Gerty blurted out.

'Don't be ridiculous. Why would they put a dangerous wardrobe in my bedroom?' Alice said smugly.

'It's not your bedroom, it's our bedroom and Gerty's right, so don't open it,' Stef said.

'Why should I believe you?'

'Because you don't want to end up with a first offence and a wart on your face, do you?' Stef grinned.

Alice rubbed her freckly nose before she walked back over to her bed and put her pile of clothes down onto it.

'There's a drawer under your bed,' Charlotte said.

Alice nodded before sitting on her knees and pulling the drawer out. She studied it before reluctantly unpacking her case and placing her clothes inside.

Once everyone had finished unpacking an awkward silence fell over the room and no one seemed to know what to say or do.

'Why don't we all tell each other a little bit about ourselves?' Charlotte suggested nervously, breaking the silence. The other girls all nodded.

'Okay, I'll start. My name is Charlotte Smyth, I'm eleven and I only recently found out that I am a witch. I knew I could do special things that my friends couldn't do but I didn't put much thought into it, at least not until I went to a party. There was a boy who was teasing me about my hair, so I unintentionally froze him. My mom showed up and unfroze him and then she told me that she was a witch and so was I. You see my mom kept being a witch, secret from my dad, he's an ordinary and he thinks that I'm at some *normal* boarding school. Mom says he can't ever find out because he wouldn't understand. So, all this is new to me but I'm really happy to be here and have you all to share a room with,' she smiled.

'I'll go next,' Gerty said, as she hopped up and bounced from one leg to the other. 'Hi, I'm Gertrude Baggs, Gerty for short-'

'What a horrible, ugly name,' Alice interrupted.

'Shush,' Stef shot Alice a stern look.

'I like your name,' Charlotte said.

'Thanks,' Gerty smiled, unfazed by Alice's comment. 'I am ten but was accepted into this Academy a year early because I developed the skill of levitation at a very young age. Both of my parents have powers and at home I was encouraged to practice witchcraft. Up until now I've been home-schooled as I didn't fit into a normal school. It was so hard not using magic there, especially when the boys used to tease me about my last name. I may have turned a couple of them into toads,' she grinned.

'I am super excited to be here in a proper castle with real life witches and I can't wait for lessons to begin.'

'Me next,' Alice chimed in, as soon as Gerty had finished talking. 'I am Alice Smithers, from the world-famous Smithers family. You all would have heard of my family as we're well known in the magical world,' she stuck her nose into the air.

'Mommy and Daddy believe that I am extremely powerful so that's why I am here. Of course, they will miss me terribly, but I owe it to the Academy to show all of you lower rung girls how to behave like a lady.'

There were snorts and giggles from the other girls after Alice had finished talking.

'I'm Stephanie Jolly, Stef for short.'

'Jolly certainly doesn't suit your personality.' Alice really didn't have any tact.

Charlotte grabbed one of the pillows off her bed and threw it across the room at her, hitting her on the head.

'I can't believe you just did that,' Alice dropped the pillow by her side. 'I shall be keeping that pillow.'

'Give it a rest will you,' Stef grabbed a pillow off her bed and also threw it over at Alice, who only just ducked in time.

Soon everyone was holding a pillow and tossing them around, hitting each other. Laughter erupted and even Alice joined in, as she clashed her pillow against Stef's.

Gerty squealed as a pillow went flying past her head, before she picked one off her bed and flung it over at Charlotte who caught it and threw it straight back. Charlotte then grabbed one of her own pillows and joined in the pillow fight with Stef and Alice. Gerty picked up a pillow and joined in too.

'Settle down girls, you are definitely not showing refinement and you don't want to be caught for your first code of conduct,' a girl blocking the doorway said, her arms folded, another girl standing slightly behind her.

The four girls collapsed on their beds and the floor and let out bursts of uncontrollable laughter. Gerty was the first to recover from her laughing fit and walked over to the girls.

'Hi, are you both new here too?' she asked and the girl with the folded arms nodded. 'My name's Gerty, nice to meet you. What are your names?'

'I'm Margaret Montgomery and my friend is Demi Taylor, we are in the room next door and we couldn't concentrate due to the awful hullabaloo you were making,' she stared at the girls but that just made Stef laugh even more.

'We're going back to our room now, try to keep the noise down and act like grown-ups,' she flicked her hair behind her, before she left the room, Demi following along behind.

'Act like grown-ups,' Stef mimicked the girl's voice, before she flicked her own hair.

Charlotte picked up a pillow and threw it at Stef and they all burst into laughter again.

'I must do something adult-like, such as reading an educational book before dinner is served,' Stef said.

'Or get rid of the creases in the sheets,' Gerty laughed.

'Or sit here in silence and be a picture of decorum,' Charlotte sat down on her bed and crossed her legs and pouted her lips.

'Oh, how lovely and adult-like you are,' Stef laughed.

Alice couldn't hide her smile as she shook her head and picked up a pillow.

'You should be picking up all my pillows and pumping them up, seeing as you're the ones who threw them at me.'

'No chance,' Stef grinned. 'Hey, it could be worse. You could be sharing a room with Margaret Montgomery and her minion.'

'Shush, she'll hear you,' Charlotte giggled.

'You must act like a grown-up Charlotte,' Stef laughed, as she again flicked back both sides of her hair.

'Does anyone know what time dinner is, I'm so hungry,' Gerty said, putting her hand to her stomach.

'I don't know,' Stef shrugged and Charlotte shook her head.

'At home we have servants who prepare all our food and a butler who calls us into the dining hall when it's ready. The food is always exceptional, especially the caviar canapés and the baked Alaska.

'I'm happy with fries and a burger,' Stef said.

'Me too,' Charlotte said. 'With lots of mayo.'

'Marshmallow ice cream with extra chocolate sauce,' Gerty said licking her lips. 'Ah, now I'm even hungrier.'

'I don't eat burgers,' Alice said, a worried look on her face. 'I hope they have upper class food here or I will waste away. I don't eat common food, like burgers.'

'I'm sure you'll be fine,' Stef smirked.

A bell rang loudly, and they all hopped up and looked at each other excitedly, before they headed for the door.

'All witches must proceed to the meeting room,' Molly said, as she flew past their room on her purple flickered broomstick. 'All witches must proceed to the meeting room.'

Stef led the way along the hallway and down the staircase into the meeting room, which now had long tables in it, with long red and black tablecloths on them. The room was already filling up quickly with the other girls. Stef walked over to the end of an empty table and Charlotte and Gerty followed.

Alice saw that Margaret and Demi sat in the middle of one of the tables where no one else was sitting. She walked over to them and sat down next to Margaret.

'Excuse me, but you can't sit there. Don't you dare ever sit there again,' she glared at her.

'Yeah, you're too ugly and no way near cool enough to ever associate with us,' Demi smirked.

Alice fought back tears as she stood up and quickly made her way over to the spare seat next to Charlotte. No one else heard what had happened but even so, the seats next to Margaret and Demi remained empty.

The room fell silent as the Witchress and the other teachers all flew in on their broomsticks and over to the platform, that now had a long table on it. The dragon seat was placed centrally behind the table and looked even grander next to the ordinary bronze framed chairs.

Charlotte looked up at the line of seated staff, noticing how they all looked beautiful. She wondered if she'd be a teacher one day or if she'd marry an ordinary like her mom had and hide the fact that she was a witch. She didn't know the answers to these questions…but she did know that now she knew about the witching world she was curious to learn more and couldn't imagine ever going back to living as an ordinary.

'Welcome to the first dinner of this academic year, we shall start as we always do by saying the witches' creed,' Miss Moffat said.

As she began to speak, the other witches joined in:

'Witches old and witches young
owls and bats and black cats too.
Come together in this castle
to bring out the best in you.

With perfect love and perfect trust
we learn the spells and witches' rules.
Acting for the good of all
now let's eat in this great hall.'

Charlotte looked at Stef and they exchanged awkward glances because everyone else around them seemed to know the words to the creed, including Gerty and even Alice, although she only joined in on the last few sentences. Charlotte knew that she'd need to learn it for next time so that she didn't stand out and reminded herself to ask Gerty to teach it to her and Stef later.

As soon as the witches creed had finished the bats flew into the room carrying bowls of broth and baskets of bread rolls. They went to the teacher's table first before they brought in food for the girls.

Charlotte watched and she was incredibly impressed as two bats quickly but precisely placed the bowl of orangey red broth down in front of her. On seeing Stef begin to eat and Gerty grab a roll out of the basket in front of them, she also took a roll and then placed her spoon into her broth. Picking up the silver goblet in front of her, she saw that it was now full of cranberry juice, even though she was sure it had been empty when she'd first sat down.

The main course was a selection of steamed meats and freshly cooked vegetables and dessert was an array of fruits and mini cakes that the bats brought in on three tiered stands. The food was so delicious that even Alice hadn't complained once, although when Charlotte thought about it, she realized that Alice hadn't said anything since she'd sat down.

When everyone had finished eating Molly stood up and said 'luculentam' as she waved her wand. All the dirty dishes, goblets and cutlery immediately vanished, and the tables were perfectly tidy.

'I so need to learn that spell,' Stef said, and Charlotte and Gerty nodded in agreement.

'Now that dinner is over it is your free time to do as you wish, may you use it wisely. I request the new students to stay behind and Molly will give you a tour of the Academy. As for the rest of you, you're now free to leave,' Miss Moffat said. She got onto the broomstick that was floating behind her chair and led the rest of the teachers and older students out of the room.

Charlotte watched as the room became quieter. Then she followed the others over to where Molly was standing in front of the platform, her blonde-hair now tied into bunches.

'I don't see why I need a tour, I know where my room is, and the meeting hall is easy to find. Surely servants should be on call to show me the remaining rooms as and when I need to see them,' Alice said, breaking her short bout of silence.

'This castle is huge and I'm excited to see more of it,' Charlotte whispered to Gerty.

'Me too.'

'Welcome to Miss Moffat's Academy, I think I've already met the majority of you but for those of you who don't already know me, I am Molly McDonald, head prefect. If you have any questions or problems then my room is on the third floor, it says head prefect on the door so you can't miss it. I'm happy to help you all out-'

'You get you own room?' Alice rudely interrupted.

'Yes, I do but I had to share a room when I was your age. If you are insistent on having your own room, then study hard and maybe when you're in your final year here, you too will become a prefect.'

'Fat chance,' Margaret whispered snidely which caused Demi to giggle.

'This castle is a labyrinth of hallways and staircases, so it is important to get your bearings. Although if you find yourself lost and alone then simply call out to the bats and they will come and help you. There is much to see so let's begin,' she stepped forwards and the girls that had been surrounding her stepped aside, creating a pathway for her to walk through.

They followed Molly out of the meeting hall and into the depths of the castle.

Chapter Six

The first room they were taken to was the huge laundry room, full of loud, spinning washing machines. Charlotte was surprised that this room looked quite normal and that the clothes didn't magically wash themselves.

'This room is only for your uniforms and ordinary clothes, your formal capes and witch's hats will be collected and washed by the Academy staff after each formal occasion and returned the following morning,' Molly said.

'Excuse me but where are the dryers?' Alice asked.

'Erm, the sun,' Molly pointed out of the window at several long clotheslines.

'What, we have to carry our wet clothes all the way out there and hang them up ourselves?'

'Yes, you do.'

'That's an outrage, I am from the famous Smithers family, I can't be expected to do such a thing. I insist that the servants do my washing for me and carry it outside.'

Molly waved her wand in the air and pointed it at Alice as she said, 'Strideo!' Alice immediately shrunk down and her clothes fell into a pile on the floor. A squeaking sound came from within the pile of clothes and a white mouse with brown patches on it scurried out by Stef's feet, causing her to let out a shriek and jump back.

'I probably shouldn't have done that, but she was driving me crazy,' Molly shrugged and all the other girls looked at her…shocked.

Charlotte bent down and picked up Alice, cupping her in her hands.

'That will shut her up for a while,' Margaret said to Demi and they both sniggered.

'It's probably best you keep hold of her, so she doesn't get trampled,' Molly said, as she walked towards the door.

Gerty bent down and bundled up Alice's clothes, before she followed the others.

'We shall visit the common room next,' Molly said, after she stopped in front of one of the restrooms. 'But first things first,' she took the bundle of clothes out of Gerty's hands and threw them into the rest room before she carefully took Alice out of Charlotte's hands and peered down at her.

'Alice, your whining attitude has to change. If it doesn't I'll turn you into a slug next time.' She stepped into the rest room and lowered Alice onto the ground, before she waved her wand and said, 'Exero,' and then closed the rest room door.

About a minute later a sheepish looking Alice appeared out of the rest room, readjusting her dress.

'Right then, the common room it is,' Molly said, before she continued up the hallway.

The common room was as large as the meeting hall and just as impressive with its marbled floor and high ivory white ceilings. It was full of girls playing various games and Molly walked them over to a table-tennis table. Instead of bats, the girls used their wands and instead of a ball, there was a large, fuzzy bumblebee. When the girls playing hit it, it buzzed loudly, and their wands flashed.

Charlotte didn't care much for bees, she'd stepped on a dozing one once and it had caused her foot to swell. On learning that the bee would have died after stinging her, she'd found herself feeling guilty, even though her foot hurt for about a week afterwards.

Molly paused in front of some girls playing limbo under a trail of hairy stinging caterpillars. A shorthaired girl didn't lower herself enough and brushed her arm against one of the caterpillars. The part of her arm that had touched the caterpillars began to turn green and her hair floated straight up. The girl looked mortified, before rushing off to the rest room.

There was laughter from new girls, but the older ones went

back to playing limbo with little reaction at all.

'Will she be okay?' Charlotte asked.

'I've told Hetty a hundred times to bend lower, she'll be fine in twenty-minutes,' Molly replied.

Charlotte nodded but made a mental note never to play that version of limbo.

There was laughter coming from the other side of the room, so Molly led them over to it. There was a large picture of a fierce looking green dragon.

'They are playing put the pin on the dragon's tail,' Molly said.

A tall, slim girl placed a blindfold over her eyes and the girl by her spun her around before she reached out her hands and cautiously moved closer to the painting, then stuck a pin into the dragon's tummy.

The painting let out a loud roar that startled the new girls. The girl who was having a turn, was given the pin back. After being spun around once more, she had another attempt, but this time she placed the pin on the dragon's neck. Once again, the painting roared.

'Last chance,' one of the girls said and the others giggled.

Taking more care, the girl hesitated and then placed the pin on the dragon's leg. There was no roar at all, and the girl took off the blindfold to see how accurate she'd been. Immediately the dragon came to life and became 3D as it stepped out of the painting and spat fire at her, causing her to jump back as the other girls laughed.

'Sorry.' The girl patted the dragon on its head, which it shook before it went back over to the painting and stepped back into it.

All the new girls behind Molly had moved quickly back, startled by what had taken place. Charlotte was both fascinated and terrified at the same time and wondered what she would stumble upon next.

'I won't be playing that game,' Gerty announced.

'I don't want my hair to be singed,' another girl with long curly red hair said.

'As you can see, you only get three chances and if you miss all three, well then you should be prepared,' Molly grinned. 'These may seem like games, but this is where you can practice and refine your skills.'

'I thought games were meant to be fun,' Stef whispered to Charlotte.

'You're a chicken, cluck, cluck,' Margaret sniggered.

Stef looked annoyed but she ignored Margaret and instead focused on Molly.

'Enough of this room, next on the tour is the grand library,' Molly beckoned them to follow her. She walked across the room with the sound of the dragon roaring behind them.

The library was crammed to the high ceilings with row-upon-row of books and a musty old book smell filled the room. To Charlotte it resembled a Victorian library and stepping into it was like going back in time. There wasn't a computer or any sign of modern technology in sight and even the large oak tables looked aged and worn.

'The Mistress of the Books is busy, so we have to wait here,'
Molly whispered, as she gestured with her eyes over to
where two attractive women were standing in conversation
with each other.

Feeling impatient and not understanding why they needed
the librarian to talk to them about reading books, Stef
walked over to one of the shelves and picked a book up.

A face appeared on the cover of the book and said, 'How to
Use Herbs in Potions by Roberta Mayfield.'

'Shi...vers,' Stef shouted out, dropping the book.

Before she could fully comprehend what was going on she
was lifted off her feet up into the air and then turned upside
down so that yet again her holey knickers were on display to
everyone.

All the girls giggled, even Charlotte who tried to disguise
her laughter under her hand.

'Young lady, never drop any of my books again. This is my
kingdom and I am a ruthless leader. These books are mostly
hundreds of years old and they will be treated with respect,'
a woman with long mahogany colored hair said, her stern
voice seeming too severe for her youthful appearance.

Stef's face turned a beetroot shade of red from a mixture of
the blood pooling to her head as well as her embarrassment.
She tried holding her dress over her knickers, but it wasn't
an easy thing to do as she was feeling dizzy and nauseous.

'S-sorr-.'

'Just don't do it again,' she waved her wand and Stef turned the right way round and landed back on her feet, holding her pounding head and trying to ignore the large smirks on Margaret's and Demi's faces.

'My name is Mistress of the Books and this is my library. I am not here to be your friend, but I am here to assist you with your book choosing if you should need it. This library is a place of great learning and knowledge and you will treat everything in here with the utmost of respect,' she straightened her velvet black hooded cape.

'There will be NO misbehavior in MY library. If you make too much noise or are disobedient in here, then I shall have no hesitation in turning you into a toad. Do it again and I will send a needle and cotton to sew up your mouth. I know every single one of these books from cover-to-cover and I will make sure that they are all respected. I am always watching, and I see everything that goes on in this library...everything!' she said, staring at Stef.

'The books have no words or pictures on the cover, and they are all very old and all surrounding different aspects of witchcraft. When a book is picked up a face appears on it and the book announces its title, as you already know,' she shot Stef another stern look, causing Stef to look at the floor and hope that she wouldn't be lifted upside-down again.'

'Some pages have words but many of them have images that come to life and talk to the reader. There are two sections in this library, the common section that you can all access,' she gestured around her. 'And the restricted section,' she pointed to further down the room where a section of shelves was roped off. 'You are NEVER to go into the restricted area,' her eyes darkened. 'That section is only for staff and for students in their final year.'

'Choose which book you want out of these drawers,' she led them over to a wall of wooden drawers, all with various categories labeling them.

The highest drawers had an image of a skull on them. 'NEVER go near the restricted drawers, told apart by the skull on them. There will be dire consequences if these are ever tampered with.'

'Look up what you want to read about and choose a card,' she opened a drawer with 'common pets for witches' written on it and pulled out a card. 'The book will come to you,' a book wedged itself off a nearby shelf and flew over to her, landing in her hand.

'*How to Train Your Toad* by Cassandra Jemina Woodley,' a voice said, after a face had appeared on the book cover.

'When you've finished with the book put it down on this shelf on your way out,' she gestured to an empty shelf that was close to the door. 'Books must NEVER leave the library and you must sit down at a table to read them. They are fragile and very old so treat them with the care they deserve.'

Then she narrowed her eyes and stared at all the girls, 'Remember, even if you can't see me I'll be watching you. And no loud noises in the library are tolerated, witches are here to learn.'

Her face turned even darker and she bent down towards them. 'At the far end of the library hall there is a huge wooden door with a dragon handle,' her tone was low and serious. 'Nobody except for Miss Moffat and myself are allowed to enter through this door. The Book of the Dragons is behind it, a book so dangerous that the door is protected by a powerful spell. You must never go anywhere near this door as it would put your life in great jeopardy!'

'That will be all, I best get back to my books. I shall no doubt see you all shortly,' she said, before she walked away from them.

'Right, let's continue the tour,' Molly whispered.

All the girls remained silent until they had left the library, even Alice who after having seen what the Mistress of the Books had done to Stef knew better than to test her.

'She was terrifying,' Stef whispered to the girls, as she rubbed her head. 'I wonder what her real name is. Miss Mean Mistress?'

'Mistress of Misery,' another girl chimed in.

'Mistress Miserable,' Gerty chuckled.

'I'd advise you all to be quiet,' Molly said.

'But we aren't in the library anymore,' Stef said.

'I suggest you always do the right thing, unless you want to be turned into a toad for the day.'

Some of the girls looked over their shoulders and back at the library entrance. No more was said about the Mistress of the Books, but Charlotte couldn't stop thinking about the library. She liked books, always had, but she was worried about going back in there. What if she accidentally dropped a book or what if a restricted book card was in the wrong drawer and she accidentally pulled it out? It was definitely the scariest library she'd ever been into.

'Last up is the flying arena,' Molly said, as she stopped by two large bronze doors that were on the ground floor.

They followed her out into a large courtyard, overlooked by vine-covered walls.

'Here you will be taught by Miss Firmfeather, one of the most accomplished flying instructors in the world.'

'When do we get our broomsticks?' Alice asked.

'Miss Firmfeather will meet with you tomorrow and tell you all about the flying program. As for your broomsticks, you'll be getting them tomorrow but whether you can fly on them or not will be up to Miss Firmfeather.'

There were excited murmurs between the girls at the prospect of soon being able to fly.

'Excuse me but won't we be hurt if we fall off?' Charlotte asked, as she stared at the hard-looking ground.

Molly smiled as she jumped up into the air then landed back down on the ground which became bouncy beneath her feet.

'I don't need a soft surface to land on because I've had lessons from my father, so I will simply blitz through the flying lessons,' Margaret said loudly.

Molly gently shook her head but didn't respond, a faint smile on her face.

Charlotte was definitely more excited about flying than she was about going back into the library. Especially now that she knew she would bounce off the ground if she fell off.

'You've all had a huge day today but tomorrow will be even more exciting, so you all need to go back to your rooms and get ready for bed,' Molly said, as she walked towards the doors.

Charlotte took one last look at the flying arena and wondered what it would be like to soar around it on her very own broomstick, before following the group back into the castle.

Back in their room they were excitedly discussing the tour,

and how they couldn't wait for flying lessons and how they'd help each other out when doing laundry. Charlotte and Gerty knew better than to mention Stef being turned upside-down or Alice being turned into a mouse, and instead they tried to keep the conversation bright.

'This can't be correct,' Alice shouted from the bathroom. 'Why is there only one? I can't be expected to share a bathroom, I need my own.'

'Seriously, at home I have to share a bathroom with my two older brothers, my little sister and my parents so I don't know what you're whining about,' Stef said.

'I shouldn't be expected to share a bathroom with common girls.'

Stef looked at Charlotte and Gerty and winked and they smiled back before Stef grabbed Alice, followed by the others, who lifted her up into the bathtub.

'Let me go this instance,' Alice squealed out, as she swatted her hands against them.

Stef turned the cold tap on, soaking Alice.

'It's okay Alice, we're at your service,' she giggled.

'You wait till my parents here about this,' she grunted.

'Would you like some more water madam,' Stef laughed.

'No, I would not,' Alice snapped, before she splashed at them.

Soon they were all laughing, even Alice.

'This bathroom's pretty big,' Stef looked around her. 'We could all use it at the same time if we wanted too,' she grinned.

'There is no chance of us doing that,' Alice said and Stef laughed.

They all dried themselves off and got ready for bed. When Stef turned the bedroom light off she had to stumble her way over to her bed, all the while moaning about the need for a wand so she could turn the light off magically.

Charlotte pulled the covers up to her face and closed her eyes. That's when she heard sniffling sounds and a smothered cry. She crept out of bed and tried to navigate herself over to where the sounds were coming from…Gerty's bed.

'Are you okay?' she whispered, as she gently pulled the covers off Gerty's face.

'Yes,' she sobbed. 'I'm just missing my mom and dad.'

'Come over to my bed and have a cuddle,' Charlotte said, and Gerty nodded before she followed Charlotte and got under the covers.

A few minutes later Gerty was asleep and breathing softly, so Charlotte quietly got out of her bed and tip-toed over to Gerty's.

She thought about the day she'd had. It had been an intense one, but it had opened her eyes to a whole new world, one which brought with it much excitement. She was eager to start lessons and learn more about this Academy. But most of all she was glad that she'd made new friends, even Alice with her annoying snobbish ways. She liked all her roommates and she liked it here. Her last thought before she fell asleep was that it was going to be all right in this place. She was a witch, and this was where she felt she belonged.

Chapter Seven

There was a loud hooting sound and at first Charlotte pulled the covers over her head and carried on dreaming. The hooting continued and realization of where she was becoming apparent. She kicked the covers off and rubbed her eyes, before pulling herself up in bed and seeing a brown owl perched on the window ledge, it's head cocked in her direction.

'An owl as an alarm, I've never heard of anything so stupid,' Alice said, as she pulled her fingers through her knotty hair.

'Fitness training in thirty-minutes,' the owl hooted, as it moved from one leg to the other.

'What about breakfast?' Stef asked.

"Fitness training first. Breakfast will be served after that. Head for the grassy area through the common room in thirty-minutes.' The owl hooted once more before flying off out the window.

'Wait, come back,' Alice jumped out of bed and rushed over to the open window, peering out at the clear sky. 'This is an outrage, I am here to learn witch skills, not to win a triathlon.'

'I like sport,' Gerty said, as she scrummaged through one of the drawers under her bed and pulled out her jogging pants. 'I play tennis with my dad sometimes,' her face suddenly fell. 'Oh no, you don't think this fitness lesson will involve bumblebees as balls do you?'

'Only one way to find out,' Stef grinned, noticing that Alice had moved towards the bathroom. She raced forwards and barged past her, locking the bathroom door behind her.

'I will be sure to report you for this,' Alice bashed on the door.

Charlotte tried to hide her smile by looking down into one of her drawers. She contemplated what to wear, deciding on a plain grey t-shirt and a pair of black shorts.

'I'm sure it'll be fine Gerty,' she said.

'I hope there's a giant bee, bigger than this room and it stings Stef on her bottom,' Alice grunted.

'I heard that,' Stef opened the door. 'Anyway, the bathroom's free,' she smirked.

'At home, every bedroom has a large en-suite and my bath is bigger than this entire bathroom.'

'Well, us common folk are used to sharing,' Stef grinned.

Alice huffed, before she stepped into the enclosure.

Charlotte was curious about what the fitness lesson would be like, she was curious about everything that came with this Academy. This whole world was new to her but at the same time it was more exciting than she could ever have imagined.

After everyone had used the bathroom, she grabbed a black zip-up jacket, and followed the others out the door and down the hallway, turning to see that Alice who was wearing an expensive looking velour tracksuit, was hurrying along behind them.

They walked through the common room and out onto the large grassy area where a group of first years were standing around a slight woman in a plain dark leotard. She was standing perfectly balanced on one leg, her long light brown hair covering most of her face, her oak broomstick laid out in front of her.

Margaret and Demi stood at the far side and sniggered when they saw Charlotte and the others join the group. Charlotte looked away from them and focused on the large object situated behind the teacher, which was a very realistic model of a fierce looking dragon.

'I hope it doesn't breathe fire like the other one did,' Stef whispered.

Charlotte was about to say that of course it would not because it wasn't real, but then she saw it move its tail. She jolted back which caused Margaret and Demi to snigger once again.

The last of the students arrived and the teacher beckoned them forwards.

'Come on girls,' her tone assertive.

They hurried forwards and joined the row of students. There were curious looks in the direction of the dragon, but no one seemed excited at the prospect of a fitness lesson, especially not Alice who was standing with her arms folded and a miserable expression on her face.

'Welcome to your first fitness lesson, I am Miss Dread and I am your fitness teacher here at the Academy. I can see by the looks on some of your faces that fitness may not be your favorite activity but that will change,' she looked at Alice. 'One day you will be in a situation where your fitness will need to kick in when your luck runs out.'

Stef stood on the tips of her toes as she rose her arm into the air.

'Yes darling?' Miss Dread asked, as she looked towards her.

'Then couldn't we just use magic?' she asked.

'Not always. Say for instance your wand broke or you were drastically outnumbered, it's always best to be prepared and being physically fit is important for all witches.'

Charlotte glanced at Alice and hoped that her own face did not look as opposed to fitness class as Alice's face did. Charlotte had always been average when it came to sport and worried if "average" would suffice with Miss Dread. She found herself hoping that their teacher was not as severe as her name suggested.

Finally bringing her leg down from her flamingo pose, Miss Dread gestured them to follow her over to the dragon. All the girls made sure there was a large space between them, and the fierce looking creature, which was staring at them with one eye opened.

'This is Dexter, the Academy's trampoline. Rest assured you won't hurt him, and he won't hurt you.'

'We can't be expected to bounce on that,' Alice said.

'It is very easy and rather fun. Here, I shall show you, she climbed up the stepladder positioned by the dragon and began to jump in the middle of the belly area. 'If you feel yourself falling off don't panic as he will catch you with his tail, tongue or claws and safely put you back onto his belly.'

She purposely jumped forwards so it looked like she was going to fall in a heap on the ground but before she could Dexter flicked out his long pink tongue and tossed her safely back up.

Miss Dread stopped bouncing and climbed down the steps, her hair falling perfectly back into place.

'Who's next?' she asked and most of the girls took a step backwards and proceeded to stare at the ground.

'Miss, I will,' Margaret stepped forward.

'Bravo darling,' she took Margaret's arm and led her over to the stepladder. 'Please refrain from bouncing on this end of Dexter,' she pointed to the lower part of his belly.

'Why?' Margaret asked, as she confidently climbed the ladder and stepped onto the center area.

'Just follow my instructions,' said Miss Dread.

Margaret didn't hesitate in jumping as high as she could, but it wasn't long before curiosity took hold and she began to jump on the southern part of the dragon's belly. Before Miss Dread had time to warn Margaret to move, Dexter let out a huge fart that caused all the other girls to laugh and swat the air in front of them as they covered their faces with their hands and sleeves. Margaret propelled high into the air and out of the dragon's grasp.

Miss Dread grabbed her broomstick and flew over to

Margaret, catching her before she fell and pulling her onto the back of the broom behind her.

'What did I tell you about following the rules?' Miss Dread asked sternly, as she landed the broomstick and glared at Margaret.

'S-sorry,' Margaret muttered sheepishly, the usual smug look disappearing from her face.

'Don't do it again or you'll be in Miss Moffat's office before you can say beetle bubble broth. That goes to all of you,' she looked over at the rest of the girls. 'Right, who's next?'

Alice immediately put her hands to her stomach and feigned a pained look.

'You,' Miss Dread pointed at her.

'I have a stomach ache, I think I need to go back to my room,' Alice cried.

'Nonsense, come on, I'll help you up,' she held her hand out to Alice.

'I really don't feel well,' she stared at Miss Dread's hand, not taking it.

'Nonsense,' Miss Dread grabbed Alice's hand and led her over to the dragon, stopping by the stepladder. She bent over and whispered to Alice, 'I know that you're scared. Trust yourself; I know you can do this.'

Alice nodded but didn't move. Miss Dread stepped in front of her and walked up the ladder.

'Follow me,' she held out her hand, which Alice promptly took, and they both stepped onto the dragon's belly together.

Leading Alice towards the center of Dexter's belly, Miss Dread grasped both her hands and they jumped, gradually going higher and higher until Alice's shrieks turned into giggles and her frown turned into a smile.

'Darling, I knew you could do it,' she gave Alice a congratulatory grin, as she helped her down off the ladder.

'Now my darlings, who is next?' Miss Dread looked warmly at the girls.

All the girls had a turn and they were all forced to admit that it was the funniest and most enjoyable fitness lesson they had ever had. A few days earlier, Charlotte would never have believed that using a dragon's belly as a trampoline was possible, but now she knew differently. This Academy had opened a door into a new world, one where anything seemed possible, and Charlotte was excited to see what would happen next.

'Darlings, darlings, fantastic, you were all fantastic!' Miss Dread pulled out her wand and made a gold medallion with a long white ribbon appear. 'I give medals out to those I feel deserve them the most and today I have a certain girl in mind,' she looked directly at Alice. 'You darling, you have shown us all that it's okay to be scared and that overlooking fear is a triumph that should be awarded.' She held the medal out to her.

Alice was unable to hide her smile as she stepped forwards and took the medal. She pulled the ribbon over her head and held the medal up so she could study it.

'Thank you girls, you're free to go. I'll see you tomorrow morning bright and early for your next fitness lesson.'

All the girls dispersed and headed back to their rooms.

'This medal suits me, don't you think!' Alice exclaimed, after they had walked into their room.

'You deserved it,' Charlotte smiled.

'You were really brave Alice,' Gerty said, as she fell back onto her bed. 'I've never bounced on a dragon before, it was definitely better than the bouncy castle I had for my seventh birthday. It got a puncture and the whole thing collapsed inwards on us all.'

'I'm sure that I'll get plenty more medals.' Alice took the medal off and laid it out proudly on her bed. 'I'm leaving it here because I don't want it to get damaged.'

'And because we have class after breakfast and the teacher might be distracted by its shininess,' Stef grinned.

'I wonder what we'll do in fitness tomorrow?'

'Dunno,' Gerty shrugged.

'I can't wait, I'm sure whatever it is, it'll be the best lesson by far,' Alice said cheerily.

'It's intriguing how you only have to give a girl a medallion and she does a total back-flip,' Stef smirked.

'You're just jealous because you didn't get one,' Alice replied.

'Yeah,' she snorted, as she searched through her drawer and

pulled out her uniform.

'My mother says we should pity those who are jealous of us because it's not their fault they were born less fortunate than ourselves.'

'You just wait until I have my wand, then the next time you make a comment like that one, I will turn you into a slug,' Stef sounded serious.

'You would get expelled for doing that,' Alice could not hide her worried look.

'It'd be worth it,' Stef grinned.

Charlotte looked down at the uniform she had laid out on her bed. It consisted of a black pleated skirt, a white blouse and a black, green trimmed cardigan with a crest that included the letters MMA written above two crossing broomsticks. It was the nicest uniform that she had ever owned, and she was eager to put it on.

They all changed their clothes as they chatted about the fitness lesson and the Academy, at the same time, wondering what they'd be given for breakfast. The bell rang to signal that the meal was ready, and they left their room dressed in their new uniforms, with excited smiles on their faces and as they headed down the hallway.

Chapter Eight

The girls walked over to the same table that they had sat at for dinner the night before and stared confused at the three flowerless plants that were set out centrally along the middle of the table.

'Do they seriously expect us to eat that?' Alice said snobbishly.

Charlotte could not hide her smile at the thought of Alice eating a plant. She looked over at Margaret and Demi who were sitting where they had last time. There was a group of older girls at the end of the table but the spaces next to Margaret and Demi remained empty.

All the staff including Miss Moffat were already sitting at the top table, each of them with the strange plants in front of them as well. The bats flew through the windows holding bowls and placing them down in front of the teachers, then more bats came in and placed bowls down in front of each of the girls. The bats flew off and soon reappeared, dropping pieces of corn into each dish.

'How can they call this a breakfast?' Stef asked.

'There's no way that I'm eating that,' Alice added.

Charlotte looked curiously down into her bowl and that was when the corn began to pop up into her face. All the girls squealed with delight and Gerty in particular, was so surprised that she almost knocked her bowl over. The bats flew above them with jugs full of milk while the girls shrieked loudly and covered their heads with their arms as the bats tipped the jugs. The milk flowed into their bowls like water from a tap, none of it spilling. The plants in front of them began to shake, as fresh strawberries, raspberries and blueberries grew on each.

Everyone reached out excitedly and ripped off the fruit, placing it on top of their cereal. Stef and Alice both picked up their spoons and began to eat. The room filled with clanging sounds as the spoons hit the porcelain bowls, echoing across the hall.

'Ahem,' Miss Moffat said, as she rose up from her dragon chair, her eyes fixed firmly on Stef and Alice before she led the rest of the girls into saying the witches' creed.

'Witches old and witches young
owls and bats and black cats too.
Come together in this castle
to bring out the best in you.

With perfect love and perfect trust
we learn the spells and witches' rules.
Acting for the good of all
now let's eat in this great hall.'

All eyes were on Stef and Alice who had finally realized what was going on. Both girls tried to quietly put their spoons down and swallow their food as quickly as possible. Stef began to choke and attempted to stifle the sound, reaching out for a sip of pineapple juice, the golden liquid that had magically appeared in each of the goblets. She tried to take a sip but had begun choking so much that she couldn't manage to drink any, and her face turned into a light shade of purple.

'Open your mouth,' Molly said, as she appeared by Stef's

side.

Stef opened it the best she could as Molly called over a bat, and with a wave of her wand she caused it to shrink until it was the size of a small coin. Stef looked on in horror as it flew into her mouth and down her throat, appearing a few seconds later gripping the stuck piece of cereal.

The rest of the girls cheered, and Stef looked sheepish, annoyed with herself for causing drama again and bringing negative attention to herself.

'Are you okay?' Charlotte whispered to her and Stef nodded back.

Breakfast was by far the tastiest one that Charlotte had ever had. She'd never tasted fruit as delicious before and looked on in awe as the goblets continued to refill with pineapple juice.

When the meal was finished and the staff departed, Molly, whose hair was in a side braid, addressed the girls.

'I'd like all the new girls to stay behind please, so I can take you to get kitted out with wands and broomsticks.'

Each girl smiled excitedly at the mention of the equipment they'd all be receiving. They knew that once they were in possession of such magical items, they would be well on their way to becoming experienced witches.

Following Molly into a section of the castle that they hadn't previously seen, they passed classrooms where bubbling sounds and explosions came from within. All the doors were shut so the interior of each room was hidden, which only made them all the more curious.

'What's happening in there?' Margaret asked.

'I don't know, maybe someone messed up their potion or something. Standard class antics really,' Molly grinned.

They headed along a quiet corridor until Molly paused by a lone door and chanted some spells, while giving a wave of her wand. The door clicked open and she gestured for them all to follow her. On entry they found a dim-lit, low-ceilinged room, with grey stoned walls and row-upon-row of boxed up wands.

'You must pick the right wand for your potential powers. If the wrong one is sought it will ensure that you cannot claim it,' Molly explained.

Charlotte wondered how they were supposed to find the right wand when each one was packaged and out of sight, but Molly simply smirked at the girls bewildered expressions. Then, with a flick of her own wand, dozens of wands burst from their boxes and floated in the room around them.

'When you've found the right one it will light up in your hand.' Molly gestured for the girls to go ahead.

Each of the girls went wild, chuckling as they chased after a wand. Demi was the first to find hers and Molly gave her an impressed look that caused Margaret to scowl.

Stef was trying to catch a long black and gold trimmed wand, but it kept shooting out of her reach. Gerty was trying to grasp for any wand that she could, giggling when each one shot away from her.

Charlotte did not attempt to take any of the wands; she concentrated on studying them, wondering which one would accept her. Her eyes then fell upon a plain oak wand that was floating alongside her. No one else seemed interested in it but Charlotte stood on tiptoes and reached out for it, half expecting it to fly away. Instead, however, it remained in place. Her hand firmly gripped it and immediately it glowed. She studied it carefully, noticing that close up it had orange patterns intricately carved into the wood; it wasn't plain at all.

'Great, we have two more,' Molly said, as she looked from Charlotte to Margaret who was also holding a glowing wand.

Realizing that Charlotte had found hers at around the same time, Margaret gave her a stern look then walked over and stood next to Demi.

Gerty was the next to find her wand, followed by Stef. Last up was Alice who was still chasing an elegant looking silver wand even though it kept whizzing away from her.

'That wand clearly does not want you!' Margaret exclaimed, and Demi and a few of the other girls giggled.

'Alice, some wands just aren't right for the person, regardless of their appearance,' Molly continued.

Begrudgingly Alice stopped chasing the silver wand and reached out for the one that was closest, a straight mahogany one. It glowed as she touched it and her face lit with a huge smile.

'Right then, that's your wands sorted. It is of the greatest importance that you look after your wand. Never misplace it or put it in a situation where it may break. A wand is a witch's most important item and each of you must remember that. Also, it should go without saying that you are not to use these to perform harmful or distressing spells on each other, unless you want to face your first warning or worse, be expelled.'

Charlotte looked down at the wand in her hand. It had stopped glowing, and this made its intricate patterning appear more discreet. She found herself wondering how something so small could be so powerful. Her mom must have had a wand at some point, and she wondered if she still had it, hidden away somewhere so that her dad would never find it.

'Next up are broomsticks,' Molly led them to the back of the room where there was an arched door. She waved her wand to unlock the door and the girls followed Molly inside. Like the other room, it had grey stoned walls but this one was slightly larger and its ceilings much higher. There were hundreds of broomsticks whizzing around and Stef only just ducked her head in time as one flew directly towards her.

'Broomsticks also have the power to reject you, so beware,' Molly said. As she gestured for them to find their broomstick.

Margaret instantly reached out and grabbed one, but it wriggled free of her grip and slapped her in the face before flying over to Stef, who grinned at Margaret as she gripped hold of it. Margaret scowled before looking around for another one.

A pale oak broom with flecks of green on the handle flew over to Charlotte and floated in front of her until she grabbed hold of it. Smiling widely, she held tightly onto it, feeling more and more like a witch. The broomsticks were easier to find than the wands, as they were more willing to track their owner. A plain brown broomstick floated over to Alice and she took hold of it with a huge grin.

When all the girls each had a broomstick, Molly beckoned them into the next room where a hat for every girl floated overhead.

'Uniforms must be worn for all classes but hats and capes are only for formal occasions. Please remain still as your hats will find you,' Molly looked up at the hats and then instructed them firmly. 'Find your owner.'

All the hats swirled around before swooping down and

landing on each of the girl's heads. They all let out excited gasps and squeals as they reached up and felt their hats.

'Nearly there,' Molly grinned, before she clapped her hands and the bats flew through the window. Each one carried a black cape and placed it gently on the girl's shoulders.

'You all look like little witches now but remember that you haven't been properly trained yet, so no using your wands or broomsticks until you've been taught how.'

As they followed Molly out of the room, Charlotte and Gerty smiled at each other and then looked excitedly at the wands and broomsticks that each was carrying.

Margaret and Demi hung back and were the last ones out of the room.

'This is ridiculous, I don't need lessons. I've been using a wand and flying for as long as I can remember,' she whispered to Demi, before double-checking that Molly couldn't hear her. 'Those rules are clearly for the other girls, not for us,' she smirked.

Margaret flicked her hair behind her back and straightened her hat before she followed Molly and the others along the corridors. She briefly looked down at her wand and broomstick and gave a sly smile.

Chapter Nine

They all had enough time to go back to their rooms and put away their new capes, hats and broomsticks before their first lesson.

'Where do you think we should put them, they might become creased in our drawers?' Stef asked, as she held out her cape and hat and looked around the room.

The wardrobe doors flung open and all the girls immediately jumped back, worried that they'd be sucked into it.

'Who opened that?' Alice asked, as she stared at Stef.

'Don't look at me,' Stef said, 'I was nowhere near it. '

'You could have opened it with magic,' she gestured to the wand in Stef's hand.

'Well I didn't,' she stared at the wardrobe. 'Have you all noticed how it isn't trying to suck anything in?'

The wardrobe shook and all the girl's capes, hats and broomsticks flew up into the air, whizzing towards it. Gerty's hat whipped into the air, directly from her head and Stef tried to grab onto her cape as it flew forwards. Every item disappeared into the wardrobe and it slammed its doors shut.

'Was that meant to happen?' Charlotte asked.

'I hope so. If not, we're all in trouble,' Stef replied.

'How will I be in trouble, I didn't do anything? Alice said.

'Let's worry about it later,' Stef shrugged.

Charlotte nodded, although she found herself worrying that she may never see her hat and cape again and thought of the trouble she would be in if that were the case.

'Are you girl's ready for your first lesson?' Sonya asked, as she and Silvia appeared in the doorway. 'Quickly grab your wands out of the magical wardrobe.'

The girls hesitated, unsure of the wardrobe and its mysterious powers. Silvia laughed and told the girls not to worry. 'Just make sure you only put your magical gear inside that wardrobe, you don't want to insult it with things from the ordinary world.'

They all nodded and tentatively grabbed their wands before joining the other new girls who were waiting in the corridor. They followed Sonya and Silvia and waited as they collected the rest of the girls and then led them all to their lesson.

Charlotte thought about what the lesson would involve and what the teacher would be like. The fitness lesson had been both exciting and terrifying and Charlotte wondered if all the lessons would be like that one.

Sonya and Silvia stopped outside of a classroom, the words 'Brewing Room' written on the door in black font.

'This will be your first lesson with Miss Maker,' Sonya explained. 'Lunch will be after this. Remember, if any of you get lost, call for the bats.

The two prefects stood aside and gestured for the girls to step through the doorway. Margaret and Demi pushed past the others and barged into the room first. They sat in the back row and sniggered at the other girls as they headed towards the remaining seats.

'Hello girls, come in, come in and find a spot,' an attractive young woman in a black corset and cape said. Her dark hair was tinged purple and she wore her witch's hat slightly wonky on her head.

Charlotte followed Gerty and Stef over to free seats in one of the middle rows and Alice sat down next to her. There was a small, black cauldron placed down in front of each of the seats.

'Hello girls and welcome to your first brewing lesson. I am Miss Maker, the Mistress of Brewing. I always get excited when new girls start here, as I love teaching fresh minds who are so enthralled to be here,' she smiled, as she looked around at all the girls. 'I will tell you a bit about me, I have been working here at the Academy for the past seventy-five-years, teaching young witches like yourselves how to brew potions.'

'She doesn't look that old,' Gerty whispered to Charlotte.

Miss Maker's eyes fell upon Gerty and she smiled.

Gerty looked startled, not understanding how Miss Maker had heard her. She wanted to tell the others that she must have bionic hearing, but she knew better than to say this…until they were out of the classroom.

'Beauty is skin deep, real beauty comes from within,' she said.

'So, does that mean that if we are beautiful witches inside, then we will grow up to look as pretty as you?' Alice chimed in.

Miss Maker let out a gentle laugh as she looked over at Alice.

The ordinaries have their ways but of course, they aren't as effective as ours. They have their creams and lotions and their Botox and surgeries. As a witch we don't need these painful youth makers, we can simply brew potion.'

Gerty exchanged an impressed look with the others. The thought of being as beautiful as Miss Maker for her whole life was an exciting one and she couldn't wait until she was older and had mastered the youth spell.

'So, you're saying that we'll be able to stay beautiful for hundreds of years?' Demi asked.

'Well Demi, remember that I said beauty comes from within to begin with. The potion will retain your appearance…BUT if goodness is absent from your soul and heart then there is no potion that is strong enough to save you from ageing into an old hag. Perhaps you need to carefully consider this,' she gave Demi a gentle smile.

Demi looked shocked and diverted her gaze down at her table. All the girls smirked including Margaret, who didn't even try to hide this from her friend.

'Some witchcraft is bad, and you should never practice it,

not ever. We don't teach those spells at the Academy, they are banned and for good reason. You are here to become strong, independent and capable witches and I am here to teach you how to use your powers for good.'

When you are in your senior year, I will teach you about some of these dark spells, not so you can carry them out, but so that you can try to stop them and reverse them. They are too powerful for you girls to know about. This is why you must NEVER go into the restricted area in the library, at least not until your senior year, and only then with the Mistress of the Books assisting you.'

'Miss, my mother attended this school and she told me about the door at the end of library with the dragon handle,' Margaret quipped.

'You are prohibited from going anywhere near that door, it is totally off limits and protected by a strong spell,' she glared at Margaret, her tone suddenly very icy.

'What is behind that door, Miss?' Alice asked the question they were all thinking but than none of the others dared to ask.

'I am often asked this question by new girls,' she sighed, a concerned look on her face. 'I understand your curiosity, but I shall tell you this only once. Hundreds of years ago, when the Academy first started, a witch called Dragina lived here. She was beautiful with long white hair and skin like silk. Dragina was obsessed with dragons, they were all she liked to talk about, and her free time involved ongoing research. She travelled the world looking for dragon eggs, eventually finding some and bringing them back to the Academy.' Miss Maker held onto the table in front of her, a fearful expression on her face.

'It is a long story and not one that I want to go into, but the dragons grew very large and caused mayhem. Miss Moffat, being the powerful witch that she is, thankfully brought the situation under control. The secrets to this terrible time are forever locked away in that room and that is why you must NEVER go near it.'

The girls exchanged shocked glances between each other. Charlotte wondered about the mysterious door and was curious to know what lay beyond it.

Miss Maker shook her head and instantly the dark mood that had covered the room dispelled.

'Today we are going to brew a potion to make you stronger,' she smiled, as she leaned in closer to them. 'Now, you must pay careful attention to my demonstration as you don't want to be too strong,' she chuckled.

'Right, let's begin. You'll find all the ingredients you need laid out in front of you and I shall guide you through what to do.'

Charlotte looked down at the neatly laid out items, not knowing what half of them were. She was overwhelmed and hoped that she wouldn't mess it up.

'Firstly, take a pinch of agarwood,' she picked up a small glass bowl that had what looked like shredded wood in it and she took out a pinch and added it to her cauldron. 'Two bay leaves, three hawthorn berries, which I agree are delicious but are also a very useful ingredient for potions.'

Charlotte looked from Miss Maker to Stef and then Gerty to check that she was doing it right, before she dropped the berries into her cauldron.'

'Half a long pepper and lastly a teaspoon of troll fat.'

'Yuck,' Stef said, as she looked down at the small bowl of fat.

'Yes, it is a bit gross but it's very effective,' Miss Maker said, as she walked over to the front row and paused by a cauldron that belonged to a girl with red hair. 'That looks fantastic, Patricia.'

'How does she know all our names?' Gerty whispered to Charlotte, forgetting that Miss Maker could hear them.

'Gerty, Charlotte, how are you getting on?' she smiled over at them.

'Erm, okay,' Gerty muttered quietly.

Yeah, okay I think,' Charlotte added.

'Great!' Miss Maker walked back to the front of the room. 'Now take your spoons and place them into the cauldron, careful not to splash any of the potion. Turn it in a clockwise direction twenty times, like this,' she began to turn her spoon, counting the turns aloud. 'When you've done that, carefully remove your spoon.'

'Now take your wand out and say, 'strength potion make me strong,' then add one cup of cranberry juice and stir another ten times in a clockwise direction. Pour a glass and drink up girls. This spell will only last for three hours and then your body's strength will return to normal.'

Stef was the first to drink her potion, followed by Margaret and then Demi. Charlotte and Gerty exchanged looks before they picked up their glasses and drank the liquid.

Charlotte looked down to see her arms begin to bulk up under her cardigan, until large muscles were visible.

'Look, look,' Gerty lifted her blouse up, revealing a six-pack of muscles on her tummy.

"Woah,' Charlotte said, as she looked down at her own stomach and legs and saw that they were changing too.

'My thighs are huge,' Alice said disgustedly, clutching a hold of her muscled leg.

'I feel so strong,' Gerty giggled, as she reached out and lifted Charlotte up with one hand and balanced her above her head, spinning her around like a spinning top.

'I feel weaker Miss Maker, what's happening?' Stef asked, as she stumbled and gripped onto the table for support before looking down at herself. Her arms and legs had become much smaller and she looked skinny and haggard.

There were gasps at Stef's appearance as the other girls gathered around her.

'Can you show me what direction is clockwise?' Miss Maker passed Stef a spoon.

Stef nodded as she put the spoon into the cauldron and stirred to her left.

'Oh dear,' Miss Maker shook her head. 'That is anti-clockwise, you're lucky the spell is only for three hours.'

She led Stef over to the comfy chair that was behind her desk and then addressed the other girls.

'This is a perfect example of how careful you must be when brewing potions and a great lesson for us all. Now, we have tidying up to do. Please be careful when cleaning up the cauldrons and glasses, don't forget your new strength.'

'Have you seen Demi's muscles? They're huge!' a girl with black hair pointed to Demi's arms.

Demi had taken off her cardigan as her arms had almost torn through it, revealing muscles much larger than anyone else had.

'You look like the Hulk,' Alice giggled and the other girls laughed, including Margaret.

Demi burst into tears and snorted as she tried to wipe the tears away with her fingers.

Miss Maker walked over to her and felt her muscles.

'Did you add a little too much troll fat, Demi?' she asked, which caused the other girls to laugh even more. 'It's okay, you are all new here and mistakes are expected. You will all be back to your old selves in a couple of hours.'

After the girls had tidied their area, they sat back down in their seats, still excited at their first lesson as well as their super strength.

'Miss, when will we learn a beauty potion?' Gerty asked.

'It seems that I am always asked this question. Girls, you will soon go the ball with the boys from the Wizard's Academy. I'm sure many of you already know that their Academy resides across the mountain range.' The girls began to giggle at the mention of boys. 'I am sure that you'll all want to look your best for that. And young Stef and Demi, I'm sure that you two will follow my instructions carefully for that potion.'

Both Stef and Demi looked sheepish and all the other girls glanced from one of them to the other.

'Off with you now, back to your dorms,' Miss Maker instructed. Smiling as she pretended to shoo them with her hands.

'I wonder what the boys will be like,' Gerty said, after they'd left the classroom.

'Cute, hopefully,' Stef responded with a grin. She still looked frail, but the potion was beginning to wear off.

'I hope they will be nice,' Charlotte added.

'And good looking,' Gerty giggled. 'What do you think we'll look like after we use the beauty potion?'

'I hope it gets rid of the frizz in my hair.' Charlotte grabbed hold of one of her curls and tugged on it with disgust.

'Mine too,' Gerty agreed.

'And mine,' Stef added.

'I hope it dulls down my freckles,' Alice said hopefully.

'I can't wait,' Gerty said, the excitement bubbling through her veins.

'Me neither,' Stef replied.

'Or me,' Charlotte said smiling.

'Or me,' said Alice.

'Do you think there's a potion to make time hurry up?' Gerty asked, the curiosity filling her features.

'There might be,' Stef responded confidently. It seemed to her that there must be a potion for just about everything.

'Miss Maker said the ball was soon, so we shouldn't have to wait long,' Charlotte looked thoughtfully at the others, all the while imagining the excitement that lay ahead.

Deep in conversation, they walked back to their room, each girl in good spirits at the prospect of a school ball where there would be boys, music and possibly even dancing.

***

On hearing that their next lesson was flying, the girls had felt anxious about how to get their broomsticks out of the wardrobe without the prefects there to watch over them. To their surprise as soon as they had entered the room, the wardrobe spat their broomsticks out at them.

After lunch, Miss Firmfeather greeted her new students by whizzing around the flying arena on her broomstick.

They watched in awe as she did loop-the-loops and then stood-up and balanced on it.

'That was amazing,' Gerty said to the others, as she clung tightly onto her broomstick.

'Hello girls,' Miss Firmfeather smiled, as she balanced on her broom in front of them, her arms casually folded. 'I am Miss Firmfeather and I shall be teaching you how to fly your broomsticks. Flying has always been my favorite part of being a witch and I hope that it will be yours too.

'I see that you all have your brooms and I know that you'll be eager to get started but first I need to tell you the rules.' There were moans from some of the girls. 'Rules are important and must be carried out so that everyone remains safe. Firstly, there will be no flying unless I have instructed you to do so. If I tell you to stop flying, then you will do so immediately. If you fall off, don't panic as the ground is enchanted and you will bounce off it. I want you all to enjoy these lessons but also to take your flying lessons seriously. Controlling a broomstick may look easy but that only comes with plenty of practice.'

'Miss,' Margaret shot her hand into the air and Miss Firmfeather looked at her. 'I've been flying for years, so I think I may be too advanced for this class.'

'You will have to start at the beginning just like all the other girls,' Miss Firmfeather said, sitting down crossed-legged on her broomstick. 'Flying is the gateway to new experiences and to seeing the world. I've flown to faraway lands on my broomstick and have floated above places that ordinaries have only ever read about in books.'

'There is a correct way to fly a broomstick and a safe way and I shall teach you these,' she looked at all the girls, pausing for a moment longer at Margaret.

Standing with her broom in-between her legs, Miss Firmfeather's hands gripped the broomstick in front of her and she told the girls to copy her pose.

'Great, now lean slightly forwards and then take your feet off the ground.' Miss Firmfeather took her feet off the ground and hovered on the spot.

Margaret was the first to lift her feet, looking bored as she watched the other girls nervously take their feet from the ground and grip onto their broomstick tightly as they flew up into the air.

'That's great girls, now we're going to practice going up and down,' instructed Miss Firmfeather. She demonstrated flying up and then down in a swift movement.

Most of the girls seemed to master this fairly quickly, except for a petite girl called Fiona, who kept flying higher and higher and seemed unable to figure out how to fly down.

'Wait here and keep practicing girls,' Miss Firmfeather said, before she flew up to rescue Fiona.

Margaret waited until Miss Firmfeather had flown away before she stopped flying in an up and down direction, then swooped above the other girls.

'You're not supposed to be doing that,' Stef said, as she wobbled on her broom.

'I am far more advanced at flying than you babies, she took her hands off her broom as she flew at Stef, who half-ducked, half fell onto her broom, only just managing to hang on.

'I'd say come and catch me…but as if that's ever going to happen,' Margaret smirked.

Charlotte had never been on a broomstick before, yet she was managing to fly up and down with ease. At least that was until Margaret flew into her and caused her to tumble off her broomstick and onto the ground. Thankfully, though, she bounced off.

Margaret smirked again as she flew back over to Demi and went back to flying up and down. Charlotte's arm hurt from where Margaret had flown into her and she rubbed it as she picked up her broomstick.

'Tumbles are expected,' Miss Firmfeather said as she looked at Charlotte, one of her hands holding onto Fiona's broom as she guided her down. 'With practice and determination, you'll soon master this skill,' she smiled.

Charlotte felt annoyed, she hadn't struggled with flying at all and she'd only fallen off because of Margaret. She wondered what the girl's problem was and if she would ever stop being so mean to everyone. Surely bullying was against the Academy's code of conduct.

At the end of the lesson, Miss Firmfeather flew into the air and waved at them, before she flicked out her wand and turned her broomstick into a huge rhinoceros, which she glided through the sky above the castle.

'I want to be able to do that,' Gerty said. 'Well maybe not a rhinoceros, I'd prefer a unicorn, with a shiny pink mane and a dazzling white horn.'

Charlotte nodded, thinking that all she wanted was to be able to fly without Margaret making things difficult for her.

Chapter Ten

It was the next morning and the girls were waiting outside for their fitness lesson. Alice had been going on and on about how good she was at fitness. But the others were more apprehensive about what Miss Dread might have in store for them.

When they arrived to find Miss Dread standing on her hands with her legs twisted around her head and a pile of hedgehogs to the side of her, they found themselves feeling even more concerned.

'Good morning darlings, today you shall be indulging in a game of hedgehog dodge ball,' Miss Dread said, before she untwisted herself and stood up on her feet.

'We're throwing those?' Stef pointed to the hedgehogs and Miss Dread nodded. 'But they're so prickly.'

'A little prickle won't hurt, and I find that it makes you work far harder than if it was just a normal, boring ball like the ordinaries use.'

'What do you think about this, Alice?' Stef asked, expecting her to moan.

'I think it sounds like fun,' she replied, which caused Stef to roll her eyes.

'Right girls, we'll have two teams, you darling, can be one team captain,' she pointed at Charlotte. 'And you, darling, can be the other,' she pointed to Margaret.

'You can pick first,' she gestured to Margaret.

'Demi.'

'Erm, Gerty,' Charlotte said, hoping that she hadn't offended Stef or Alice by not choosing them first.

'Stef,' Margaret smirked.

'Not the toads!' Stef shouted, which caused Miss Dread to glare at her. Reluctantly she walked over and stood beside Margaret.

'Alice,' Charlotte indicated her friend.

'Melody,' Margaret said and a girl with chin length brown hair walked over and stood by her.

'Patricia.' Charlotte nodded.

They continued to choose until their teams were full and

then they began the game.

'Begin on my clap and remember darlings, if you're hit then you're out. If one of the spikey little creatures is coming towards you, you must catch it,' Miss Dread said, before she clapped her hands together.

Margaret was the first to throw her hedgehog, hitting Patricia on the arm and causing her to squeal loudly. Charlotte picked up the hedgehog and threw it back at Margaret, but she ducked, and Demi caught it in her hands.

Charlotte managed to throw one at Stef, prickling her on her leg before she caught it. Another girl on the team threw one back but it scratched Charlotte's arm and then dropped to the ground. Charlotte was out of the game.

Alice seemed very good at dodging the hedgehogs but not so skilled at throwing them. Although she didn't complain, not once. Not even when Margaret finally managed to hit her on her side.

Stef seemed super competitive, regardless of whose team she was on, and she chucked a hedgehog at Gerty, which prickled her on her bottom.

'Ow, ow, ow,' Gerty squealed out, as she hobbled her way over to the sideline and stood next to Charlotte.

'Stef is ruthless when you get her in a team, I think you should have picked her first,' Gerty said.

'I'll remember that next time,' Charlotte grinned.

Margaret and Stef were the last girls left, so Margaret's team were declared the winners and Miss Dread handed them all a color changing sweet.

'That's it for now darlings, go and get ready for breakfast,' Miss Dread said, as she waved them all off.

'Sorry,' Stef said to Gerty, as she walked up alongside her.

'That's okay, although I never want to be on the opposite team as yours again.'

'Bleurgh,' she almost choked and Gerty looked at her oddly.

'The sweet changed to blackcurrant flavor, yuck. It's okay, because now it's changed to strawberry.'

'I hope it goes back to blackcurrant,' Gerty grinned.

'Sore loser,' Stef chuckled, emphasizing the word - *sore*.

***

After breakfast, Molly escorted them to their next lesson, and they entered the classroom to see a stunningly beautiful woman with chestnut hair pinned elegantly back.

They all took their seats (which Gerty found difficult, thanks to Stef and the hedgehog) and looked at the woman in awe.

'She's like a fairy princess,' Gerty whispered to Charlotte.

When all the girls had taken their seats, the woman gently rose to her feet and studied each of them.

'I am Miss Scarlet, the teacher of spells. I'm sure that the majority of you have heard about the *Book of Spells*. This book contains most of the spells that exist, everything from basic spells such as lifting an object to the more advanced ones such as changing an object's appearance. During your time at the Academy we will work through this book and teach you many spells,' she was well spoken, her tone refined.

'Miss,' Stef shot her hand up and Miss Scarlet looked at her. 'Is the *Book of Spells* kept at this school?'

'Where or where not it lays, is not of importance to you. The spells that you will be studying are in the text book you will find in front of you,' she picked up a leather-bound book.

'We will be doing a spell today but first I must warn you, spell making isn't an exact science and things can go wrong. You must take my classes seriously and with the utmost respect. I know that young witches like to experiment, but you must remember the Academy's code of conduct at all times.'

'Please can you all turn to page four in your books,' she opened her textbook and held it up for them to see. 'Today you are going to learn how to use your wands with a simple throw and return spell. Your partner will be the girl closest to you,' Stef turned to look at Gerty and Charlotte to Alice.

'One of you will say 'cup go' as you throw a cup at your partner,' she held up a glass cup. 'The other will flick their wand out in front of them, like this,' she tightly held onto her wand as she gave it a stern flick in front of her. 'Whilst you are doing this, you need to focus on how you want the cup to stop. View your wand as a barricade that's there to protect you.'

'You,' she pointed at a worried looking girl in the front row. 'Please throw your cup at me whilst saying 'cup go.'

The girl nodded, she stood up and said the words 'cup go,' as the cup flew towards the teacher. Miss Scarlet flicked her wand out swiftly in front of her and the cup stopped abruptly and fell to the ground, where it bounced off the hard floor and flew back to the thrower.

'That's how it's done. Now it's your turn. Remember what I

said about focusing on your wand. The strongest witches are those who successfully know how to channel their wands. You must think of your wand as an extension of your mind and body.'

Alice shrieked as a cup hit her head but on her third attempt, she managed to stop the cup in front of her, a huge smile on her face.

Stef and Gerty were struggling and neither of them could seem to master this spell. Miss Scarlett went over to them and demonstrated how they needed to flick out their wand.

Charlotte glanced at Margaret, who had stopped the cup every time. She looked bored. Seeing that Miss Scarlet was distracted with Gerty and Stef, Margaret used her wand to fill her cup with dragon's wee.

'Empty yourself over Charlotte's head,' Margaret said to the cup, smirking as she watched it whiz across the room, stop over Charlotte's head and then soak her in the foul yellow liquid.

Charlotte shrieked out and watched as the cup flew back to Margaret who stood there smirking.

'Oops,' she feigned an apologetic look.

'What is going on?' Miss Scarlet asked sternly.

'It was an accident,' Margaret replied innocently.

'You can escort Charlotte back to her room so that she can change her clothes.'

'It was only a bit of liquid, it's not like it has hurt her.

Besides, I want to be here for the lesson.'

'This is not up for discussion and may I suggest that you use this time to think about your behavior as I can assure you that I shall not tolerate disobedience,' Miss Scarlet glared, the annoyance evident on her face.

Charlotte and Margaret did not say a word to each other as they walked towards Charlotte's room. Charlotte was upset as she was just getting the hang of the cup spell and now she had to waste the lesson time. She was there to learn, not fall victim to Margaret's bullying games. She found herself worried that Margaret would always try to ruin things for her and result in her falling behind in her lessons.

After changing out of her wet smelly clothes and taking a quick shower, Charlotte left her room to see that Margaret was still standing outside, her arms folded. She immediately began to walk off and Charlotte followed her.

As they passed the library, Margaret unfolded her arms and forced a smile.

'Can we stop here for a bit? There's a book I want to find out about.'

Charlotte nodded, she wanted to get back to class and thought that Margaret could look for this book afterwards, but she also did not want to get on the wrong side of her. As they walked nearer to the entrance, Margaret stopped and turned to Charlotte.

'I need to be able to trust you with a secret,' Margaret said and Charlotte nodded. 'In this library is a very powerful and special book called *Salem Secrets* and it contains spells that very few witches know about. My mother told me about it and I just know that I need to find it and read it. Promise me that you won't tell anyone Charlotte, you want to be my friend don't you? You have to help me because if you tell anyone, then we'll be enemies forever.'

'I guess I could help you,' Charlotte said reluctantly, feeling trapped and nervous.

'Great,' Margaret grinned. 'You can distract Mistress of the Books whilst I find it.'

Charlotte had a bad feeling but knew that if she didn't go along with Margaret then the rift between them would only grow worse.

After seeing that the Mistress of the Books was sitting behind her desk reading a book, Charlotte walked over to her, trying to calm herself as she stopped in front of the desk and coughed to clear her throat.

'Ex-excuse me,' she squeaked, and the Mistress of the Books looked up. 'I was wondering if you could help me, you see my dad is an ordinary and I have no idea on even the most basic skills of witchcraft.'

The Mistress of the Books looked impressed at Charlotte's diligence and desire to learn. Standing, she walked around the desk and smiled.

'Of course, follow me,' she led Charlotte over to the beginners' section of the library and pulled out a book.

'*Newbies Guide to Witchcraft* by Gloria Arlington,' the book boomed.

'Now this book has everything you need to get you started.

It also explains magic to you in a non-confusing way and I highly recommend it,' she held it out to Charlotte. 'Follow me, there are plenty more books I can find for you.'

Whilst this was happening Margaret entered the library and sneaked across the room before she crawled her way over to the restricted area. She grabbed a worn looking black leather book. '*The Darkest of Spirits* by Garrent Worthington,' it announced. She looked over her shoulder before she put it back and grabbed another one. '*Desiree's Dark Magic,* by Desiree Penelope Fancroft.'

Margaret felt frustrated, she didn't have much time and she couldn't find the book she was looking for. She held her wand out in front of her and looked at it.

'*Salem Secrets* come to me, quickly now so I can see.'

Flames appeared, engulfing a whole section of books in a heat of embers and scarlet flames.

Whilst the Mistress of the Books was pulling out a book, Charlotte looked over her shoulder to see the back of Margaret hurriedly leaving the library. She looked over to the restricted area and saw a shadow of smoke appearing. Rushing quickly over there, she was horrified to see that flames were burning some of the ancient books. She tried to put out the fire, wafting the flames with her hands…but this only seemed to make them worse.

The Mistress of the Books looked up and saw what was happening. Aiming her wand at the flames, she chanted a spell. The flames disappeared and the books appeared undamaged.

'You,' the Mistress of the Books glared at Charlotte

accusingly.

'I didn't do it,' her voice was timid.

'To the head witchress' Office NOW!'

***

Charlotte had spent the last few hours stuck in a dark, windowless room. It contained a hard-looking bed and an old wooden chair, which she sat on, hoping that she wouldn't be in there long enough to need use of the bed. Tapping her fingers against its frame, she wondered what would happen to her.

Charlotte knew that she'd been stupid, of course. Margaret would not have stayed around to take the blame. Now Charlotte was in serious trouble whilst Margaret was no doubt carrying on without a care for the mess she'd caused. Charlotte should have refused to distract the Mistress of the Books. Instead, she should have simply returned to class. She didn't need Margaret as a friend, she'd always known that, which made what she had done even more foolish.

If they expelled her for this, then what? Would she end up at Witchery College or would she have to go back to an ordinary school? She did not want to leave the Academy and her new friends, she liked it there and she wanted to stay. But she also didn't want to tell on Margaret.

The door creaked open and a woman wearing a smart black fitted suit appeared.

'Charlotte, Miss Moffat is ready to see you now,' she pressed her finger to the thin black framed glasses that were perched on the edge of her nose. Charlotte presumed that they were more for fashion than for practicality, as she'd seen no other staff member wearing glasses.

Charlotte nodded, before following her out of the room, blinking her eyes to adjust to the light. The woman led her over to Miss Moffat's office and held the door open for her, gesturing for her to step inside.

Miss Moffat sat in a large black leather armchair behind an extravagant looking mahogany desk. Molly and the Mistress of the Books were sitting on a small couch at the far side of the room, and on a chair in front of the desk was Charlotte's mom.

'Charlotte, take a seat,' Miss Moffat gestured to the empty chair, and Charlotte moved towards the seat alongside her mother.

Her mom looked at her, but Charlotte glanced away, feeling embarrassed. She could not look her mom in the eye and see how ashamed she was.

'It is important you know that lies will not be tolerated in my office,' Miss Moffat said sternly and Charlotte nodded. 'Now tell me, Charlotte, what happened?'

'Erm, I don't know,' Charlotte muttered.

Her nose instantly grew half an inch longer and Charlotte was horrified to find that when she glanced down, she could easily see the sudden extension.

'I'll ask again Charlotte. Remember, lies are unacceptable and will not be tolerated. So, tell me. What happened?'

'I'm really not sure, Miss Moffat,' she said, and her nose

instantly grew longer.

'I will give you one more chance to tell the truth,' she leaned in closer to Charlotte, the anger alive in her eyes. 'If your nose grows again then you shall be expelled from my Academy.'

'Go on Charlotte, tell us what happened,' her mom encouraged, a pleading smile on her face.

Charlotte did not want to anger Margaret, but she also did not want to face expulsion. She had begun to love the Academy and she was desperate to stay.

'I think, no I'm pretty sure that Margaret did it.'

'Do you mean Margaret Montgomery?' Miss Moffat asked.

'Yes,' Charlotte lowered her head and her nose reduced by half.

'Why was she in the restricted area?' the Mistress of the Books jumped in, a concerned look on her face.

'Remember that you have no more chances,' Miss Moffat added.

'She was looking for a book in the restricted area,' she blushed, and her nose returned to normal. She reached up and touched it, relieved that it had gone back to its regular size.

'And what was your involvement, Charlotte?' Molly asked.

'I was supposed to distract the Mistress of the Books whilst Margaret looked for the book.'

Mistress of the Books was standing there staring at Charlotte, holding one of the books from the reserved section. 'You mean to tell me that your story of being behind all the others in witchcraft, and wanting some extra help, wasn't true?' Her tone tasted of outrage. 'You were using me young lady and I'm very, very, very cross with you!' Immediately her hand erupted into a ball of flame.

'I'm so s-sorry,' Charlotte burst into tears, terrified. 'I shouldn't have done it, I'm really sorry.'

Miss Moffat used her wand to extinguish the flame in the librarian's hand. 'Why did you do it Charlotte?' It doesn't seem like you to deceive someone.'

'Margaret asked me to. She said that if I didn't, we'd always be enemies. I was scared of getting on her bad side. I find her intimidating and we are in every class together.'

Miss Moffat let out a sigh, before she turned to Molly.

'Please can you take Charlotte back to her room? She shall remain there for the rest of the day.'

Molly stood and waited by the door as Charlotte scraped her chair back and got to her feet. Her mom gave her an unhappy look but still pulled her into an embrace and kissed her on the top of her head.

'This is out of character for my daughter,' she tried to explain.

'Don't worry too much. It seems to me like a case of peer pressure. It seems as though she has learned a lesson the hard way.'

Charlotte's mom let go of her and she walked over to Molly, giving her mom one last apologetic glance and receiving a smile back, before she left the room.

***

For the rest of the day Charlotte lay face down on her bed and sobbed into her pillow. She pretended to be asleep when the other girls returned from their last class for the day. She didn't want to have to explain what had happened.

She thought that they'd be gossiping about it all, but instead she overheard them say between themselves that they hoped she was okay. Even Alice didn't have anything horrible to say, which made Charlotte quietly sob even more. These girls were her true friends, not Margaret.

'Charlotte, I have a message for you,' an owl hooted, as it

perched on the windowsill.

Charlotte rolled onto her side and pulled herself up into a sitting position, her legs hanging over her bed as she rubbed her sore, bloodshot eyes before looking towards the owl.

'You're allowed to leave the room for dinner.'

'It's okay, I don't feel much like eating.'

'You will want to come, there's a very special announcement that you won't want to miss.' It gave her one last look before it flew off.

'Come on Charlotte, you need to eat.' Gerty said, walking over to Charlotte and putting her arms around her.

'But everyone will be staring at me.'

'If they do, I'll turn them into a toad,' Stef grinned, pulling her wand out and pretending to cast a spell.

'Then you'd get into trouble,' Gerty giggled.

'Well, we'll protect you some other way, after all we are your best friends.' At that moment, Stef could never have realized how those words had touched Charlotte's heart.

'Okay,' Charlotte gave a slight smile. 'I'll come.'

'Great, then let's get going, I'm hungry,' Alice responded, as she hurried towards the door.

'The bell hasn't rung yet,' Gerty said, but as soon as she'd finished speaking the bell began to ring.

'About time, we never had to wait like this at home,' Alice complained, before stepping out of the room, followed by everyone else.

When Charlotte entered the dining hall, some of the other girls were staring at her and gossiping. She looked at the ground and tried to block them out.

'They'll have something else to talk about soon,' Gerty said.

'Yeah, besides, they're more concerned with what has happened to Margaret,' Stef added.

'I heard she's been expelled,' Alice piped up.

'I heard they sent her to the bad witches' school,' Gerty said, excitedly.

'No, she's been turned into a toad and put into the school's lily pond,' Stef grinned, and Charlotte couldn't help but chuckle.

They took their seats in the grand hall and Charlotte looked over at where Demi was...sitting alone, depressed and vulnerable. Margaret was nowhere in sight. Her absence only making the gossip about Charlotte increase.

The room fell silent as Miss Moffat flew in on her broomstick. Instead of going over to her usual place on the platform, she stood in front of the top table and faced the students.

'I need to talk to you girls. Today, I am shocked and saddened to say that one of our new students, Margaret Montgomery broke our Code of Conduct in the worst possible way. I will not go into her misdemeanor, but I will say that what she did was completely unacceptable. I could hear you all gossiping on my way to the great hall and no, she is not a toad. Ladies, it is time to stop gossiping and spreading stories.'

They said the witches' creed and then hundreds of plates flew through the windows and landed on each of the tables. There were shrieks and squeals as dozens of red spotted spiders appeared on the ceiling above each table and began to weave spaghetti onto each of the plates. Charlotte shuddered but didn't say anything, she'd never been keen on spiders.

A leprechaun in a baseball shirt and cap appeared in the corner of the room and hit meatballs onto everyone's plates with lightning speed, before he did a little jig and then vanished. Just when the new girls thought that things could not get crazier the bats flew in through the windows carrying jugs of Bolognese sauce and poured it onto each of the girl's bowls.

'Do you get your food delivered to you like this?' Stef asked Alice, before she put a whole meatball into her mouth.

'Of course not,' Alice said snobbishly, as she cut a meatball in half and waved it mid-air. 'Although I do have to admit that this dining hall is much more fun than being served by servants at home.'

Charlotte looked around her at all the chatting, laughing girls. No one was looking at her anymore, each girl was too preoccupied with her food and how it was being served. This place was magical, and she never wanted to leave.

As soon as the girls left the room Stef began to gossip about Margaret, only her words came out in an unrecognizable language. She tried again but once more, her words made no sense.

When some of the other students tried to talk about Margaret their words also sounded gibberish and the corridors were filled with what sounded like a bizarre version of Chinese whispers.

'I give up, Miss Moffat must have put a spell over us all or something,' Stef sighed. 'Oh well, I'm sick of hearing about Margaret anyway.'

Charlotte didn't say anything, but she was secretly glad as she didn't want to think about Margaret or where she was and the fact that no one was able to talk about her made this easier. Miss Moffat had given her another chance and she had to make the most of it, not dwell on the past. She was a witch and this Academy was where she was meant to be. There was no more room for errors or foolishness, from now on Charlotte was determined to study hard and prove that she deserved to be there.

***

The next week carried on as normal. The girls settled into their daily routines, they learned new spells, and their friendships grew closer. Demi continued to act lost without Margaret, sitting by herself at meal times. Although she had begun to talk to the other girls a bit, Stef and Alice didn't have much to say to her and Demi ignored Charlotte as she blamed her for Margaret's disappearance. Gerty, with her huge heart, felt sorry for her and spoke to her in passing.

Breakfast had just finished, and Charlotte realized that she'd left her wand in her room, so she hurried back to get it. She grabbed it from the wardrobe and was about to leave when she turned to see Margaret standing in front of her, her arms folded and a fierce look on her face.

Charlotte tried to step past her to escape through the door. The door slammed shut. She reluctantly turned back to look at Margaret, knowing that she had no choice except to see what Margaret wanted. She was far more advanced with spells than Charlotte was.

'We need to talk,' Margaret glared, uncrossing her arms and revealing the wand that she grasped tightly in her right hand.

Charlotte looked at the door, rummaging desperately through her brain for any sort of spell that would help her.

'No one's coming to rescue you, it's just you and me,' Margaret smirked, as she took a step closer towards her.

Thank you for reading this book. I would really appreciate it
if you would leave a review…

**Witch School
Book 2 - OUT NOW!**

I hope you liked Witch Story and enjoyed following the
adventures of Charlotte and her new friends.
Can you please leave me a review?
My sincere thanks!!!!!
Katrina

Check out these other great books...

Printed in Great Britain
by Amazon